NELLIE'S QUEST

CONNIE BRUMMEL CROOK

NELLIE'S QUEST

Stoddart Kids

TORONTO • NEW YORK

*We acknowledge the Canada Council for the Arts and the Ontario Arts
Council for their support of our publishing program.*

Published in Canada in 1998
by Stoddart Kids,
a division of Stoddart Publishing Co. Ltd.
34 Lesmill Road
Toronto, Canada M3B 2T6
Tel (416) 445-3333 Fax (416) 445-5967
Email Customer.Service@ccmailgw.genpub.com

Published in the United States in 1998
by Stoddart Kids,
a division of Stoddart Publishing Co. Ltd.
180 Varick Street, 9th Floor
New York, New York 14207
Toll free 1-800-805-1083
Email gdsinc@genpub.com

Distributed in Canada by
General Distribution Services
30 Lesmill Road
Toronto, Canada M3B 2T6
Tel (416) 445-3333 Fax (416) 445-5967
Email Customer.Service@ccmailgw.genpub.com

Distributed in the United States by
General Distribution Services
85 River Rock Drive, Suite 202
Buffalo, New York 14207
Toll free 1-800-805-1083
Email gdsinc@genpub.com

Canadian Cataloguing in Publication Data

Crook, Connie Brummel
Nellie's quest

ISBN 0-7736-7469-1

1. McClung, Nellie L., 1873–1951 – Juvenile fiction. I. Title.

PS8555.R6113N452 1998   jC813'.54   C98-930052-8
PZ7C76Ne 1998

Cover and Text Design: Tannice Goddard
Cover Illustration: David Craig

Printed and bound in Canada

To my husband, Albert,
who still loves Manitoba
— where he was born and where he spent
the first forty years of his life.
My love and thanks to you
for encouraging me to write
and for being a wonderful companion.

Acknowledgements

I would like to thank Nellie L. McClung's grand-children, and especially Jane Brown-John and the Honourable John McClung for permission to use quotes from her autobiographies, *Clearing in the West* and *The Stream Runs Fast*. I would like to thank Harry Mooney, grandson of Jack Mooney, and family along with my sister-in-law Gwen Crook for showing and describing the site of the farm that was homesteaded by the Mooney family.

Thanks also to the Reference Department of Trent University Bata Library for helping me find historical background material and Nellie L. McClung's books, now out of print.

A special thanks to Dan Floyd, a teacher in Oshawa, who played with the Peterborough Junior A and Senior A Lacrosse teams, champions in

1980 and 1983 respectively for Eastern Canada. Thank you for your help with the sports chapters and also for your research into the history of the games.

1

"If you think you're gonna get away with invadin'
a man's property and privacy, you got another
think comin'! Get off, get off!"

Nellie heard the thud of approaching steps
from the other side of the cowstable door. She was
wishing more than anything that she hadn't
knocked. She had no wish to see what was going
on inside — but it was too late now.

The latch lifted and the weathered grey door
creaked open. Blinded by the dark interior, Nellie
blinked and stared straight ahead.

"I told you loud and clear — get out and get off
my land."

For Nellie, everything started to come into
focus. On the stone stoop just inside the stable
door stood a thin man with dark brown hair. One

large swatch of that unruly mop was plastered down onto his sweating forehead. His eyes were glassy and there was a leer on his face.

"Mr. Sayers, what . . . what are you . . .?"

Nellie was about to ask the farmer why he was *inside* the barn on a day that was perfect for harvesting. But fortunately, he spoke first. She was in enough trouble just being on his property.

"Well, if it isn't Miss Mooney," Sayers mumbled thickly. "And what are you doing here on my land?" He shuffled closer and stared at Nellie through narrowed eyes. He was unsteady on his feet and leaning heavily on his pitchfork. The smell of his alcoholic breath was strong.

"I've come to see Sarah, and there was no answer to my knocking at the house," Nellie said evenly, though she was trembling inside. "We've missed her at school. Has she been sick?"

"Sarah? Oh . . . Sarah, my *daughter*."

"Well, where is she? No one seems to be at the house."

"What's it to you? She's my child. I kin keep track of her."

"Well, I'm her teacher, so I keep track of her too!" Nellie's outrage was starting to overcome her fear.

"I'll send her to school when I want to, Miss Mooney, and keep her at home if I decide. So mind your own business. And get outta here before —"

Nellie looked Sayers straight in the eye. "Teachers check on their pupils these days, Mr. Sayers. After all, it's *1895*! And it *is* my business to check on the welfare of *my* pupils."

"Oh, is it your business? Well, I hear you've been going around sticking your nose in a lot of *other* people's business, too, Miss Mooney." Sayers stared back at Nellie through bloodshot eyes. "I hear you belong to the WCTU along with all those other biddies that got nothin' better to do than nag men they're not married to."

"Yes, I'm proud to be a member of the Women's Christian Temperance Union, but that's not why I'm here now."

"Oh, yeah, let's hear it for the WCTU — 'Women Continually Torment Us.' You and the old hens just don't know enough to mind your own business, do you? So just take yourself off my property right now, Nellie Mooney, or you'll wish you had."

"But, Mr. Sayers, I just —" Nellie stiffened in fear as Sayers suddenly lunged towards her, swinging his left arm to push her away. She ducked, but lost her footing and fell forward onto the stone stoop just inside the cowstable door.

"Ohhh." Nellie groaned as she felt a sharp pain in her right ankle and a stinging numbness spreading up her leg.

"Well, Miss High and Mighty, you've done it now," Sayers grinned, looking down at her. "Guess you'll have to ask for help from the likes of me."

Nellie tried to stand, but couldn't.

"Here, take my hand," Mr. Sayers said, looking at her in a more kindly way now.

Nellie tried again to stand on her own, but the pain was still too bad. She took the offered hand.

Sayers' brow relaxed, and he smiled at her. "Just

put your arm around my neck, and I'll help you over here where you can sit for a bit — right down here beside me."

Hanging onto his arm, Nellie limped to the end of the straw-covered platform between the empty cow stalls.

Sayers brushed back a little straw at the edge of the platform and pulled out an amber-coloured bottle. Beer, Nellie thought. She looked on as Mr. Sayers tipped the bottle to his lips. He was drunk already, and now he was drinking more. Pain or no pain, Nellie knew she had to get back to the door and outside. She'd been foolish to come down to the cowstable alone, she realized now. There was no one around to help her. What if Sayers became violent? And where were Sarah and her mother? Sarah had told Nellie they were planning to visit Sarah's grandparents in Ontario. But it would be strange for them to leave in September.

Nellie also knew that no one from home could help. Jack, her brother, would be too busy with the barn chores to look for her, and Mother would be preparing supper. Besides, they wouldn't even notice she was late because she often stayed on at the school on Fridays, putting lessons on the blackboard for Monday.

She stood up, but instantly sat down again. The pain left her weak and shaking. As she waited for it to pass, she realized she would have to keep Sayers talking. Then maybe he wouldn't drink any more.

"I wanted to talk to you about Sarah," Nellie began with as much confidence as she could muster. "She's a very talented child. I guess she takes after yourself in the way she reads so well."

Sayers lay back in the straw, propping himself up with one hand and tipping the bottle to his lips with the other. "Well, now, you're dead wrong there. It's me wife that reads in this family."

"You don't read at all?"

"Nah, ain't got much use for books. But I don't so much mind the wife reading when she can get her hands on one of 'em." Sayers leaned back against the tall mound of straw at the end of the platform.

"Sarah takes out books from the church library. We have quite a number now — sent from a church in Ontario," said Nellie.

"Is that so? I didn't rightly know where she got them, but if it weren't from there, it'd be somewhere else. Yup, she sure is a terror to read. Won't allow it, though, I won't, when there's work to be done — or late at night neither when there's coal oil to burn. We don't have coal oil nor money neither to burn for nothin' like that."

"But Mr. Sayers —" Nellie began, grimacing at the selfishness of this man who spent all the money he wanted drinking himself into a stupor, yet begrudged his daughter a little for light to read by. But she stopped herself from saying more. This was no time to start an argument.

Sayers tipped the bottle again, and this time he drained it. Hurling it onto a straw pile behind him, he then started pawing at a spot nearby. Nellie watched in disbelief as he brought out another full bottle, pulled the cork out with his teeth, and poured half the contents down his throat. Then, wiping his mouth with his left hand, he set the bottle down on the cement platform and turned to Nellie.

"Well, Nellie, my girl, looks like we're stuck with each other's company! You don't mind if I call you Nellie, do you?" Sayers gave a loud guffaw, then reached into his pocket for a small, curved tin flask and put that to his lips.

Nellie stood up on her good left leg and clutched the edge of the nearest cow manger. She had hopped only one step towards the door when Sayers grabbed her shoulder and pulled her back down.

Nellie gripped the edge of the cow manger again, lifted her good leg up and pushed her boot straight into the pit of Sayers' stomach. The man clutched himself around the middle and reeled backwards, yelling.

As Nellie whipped around to pull herself up, her thick, dark brown hair fell loose from its red combs and tumbled down her back. She hopped on her left leg to the door, threw it open, and slammed it behind her. Limping forward, she started for the house, but soon stumbled against a knoll, overcome with pain. She sank to the ground with a groan and trembled as she heard Sayers' low snarl right behind her.

"Miss Mooney!" someone was shouting as she raced over the top of the knoll. Nellie rolled over and slowly sat upright. On one side of her stood Sarah Sayers with her bobbed blonde hair fanning out in the warm September breeze; on the other stood her drunken father.

"Get to the house," Sayers barked at his daughter. Sarah narrowed her deep blue eyes at him, then turned and ran up the knoll towards the cabin. She was small for her eleven years, but she ran quickly.

Nellie groaned and tried to get up, standing on her good left leg. Then she turned to limp towards the house.

"Not so fast, young lady. I thought you wanted to talk to me . . . about Sarah." Mr. Sayers' voice sounded soft and kind again.

Nellie tried to control her anger as she took a slow step up the hill. But she could not hide the pain in her voice as she said, "I'm sorry to have bothered you, Mr. Sayers. I'll be on my way now." She smiled lightly and tried to appear calm. She could feel the beating of her own heart, however, and was sure Sayers could hear it pounding. She knew she had to get away from this drunken man and make her way over to her horse. There she would have to lift herself into the saddle somehow.

"Oh, yes, we have some discussing to do," Sayers blurted out. He tugged at the sleeve of her dress as if to pull her back towards the barn.

"I'm going, Mr. Sayers. Take your hand off my arm." Nellie glared at him. He dropped his eyes but got a firmer grip on her left arm and started to pull her backwards.

"Stop!" It was the sharp voice of a woman, coming from just behind Nellie.

"Mrs. Sayers," Nellie breathed with relief.

The drunken man's wife rushed forward and pulled her husband's hand away from Nellie's sleeve. "Don, please come in now," she said gently but firmly. "I have supper all ready — your favourite dessert."

Nellie looked on, half numb, as the slightly-built Mrs. Sayers whispered to her husband and stroked his arm. Her white-blonde hair had come loose at one side and her wide blue eyes, much like her daughter's, looked tired and sad. She was amazingly pale in spite of all her work in the fields.

Sayers wrenched his arm loose, swung around, and hit his wife squarely on the jaw with his left fist. She staggered back but lunged at him again before he could reach out for Nellie, who was now back on her feet and inching her way up the hill.

Mrs. Sayers grabbed her husband's sleeve, but he thrust her away. She hit the ground with such a loud whack that Nellie wondered how she could possibly rise. The woman was so small — only a tiny bit taller than Nellie, who was barely five feet.

Sayers turned to stare at Nellie, who was now pushing forward on one foot. If she were out of their way, she thought, surely their fighting would stop.

Only a little way ahead, Nellie hesitated, for she could hear the sounds of struggling. She turned and saw Sayers, close behind her, with his wife trying to hold him back. In the next instant, the man turned and hit his wife on the side of the head so hard that she crumpled to the ground. This time she lay still.

Nellie knew that there was no reasoning with Sayers now, so she turned and broke into a limping run. She felt as if a knife were piercing her ankle, but she knew she had to bring back help for Mrs. Sayers. She could hear her chestnut mare pacing at the road. How would she ever be able to untie the horse and get up on her fast enough to escape? She was still wondering how she was going to manage this when she reached the mare. But as she began to fumble with the reins, the sound of approaching footsteps stopped.

Nellie turned and looked back.

There was Mr. Sayers. He had collapsed in the dooryard and now lay on the ground, half-covered with ragweed and burrs. Nellie stood blankly staring, just when she should have been untying the mare. A loud bang came from the cabin. Nellie looked up and braced herself for the next shock. But it was only Sarah, who had run outside, slamming the front door behind her. She saw Nellie but walked bravely over to her father and stared down at him. Then she stepped around him and hurried over to her teacher.

"Pa won't bother anyone now. He'll sleep until tomorrow. And he won't remember anything that's happened. Where's Ma?"

"Your mother's hurt. Hurry! She's over near the cowstable door."

Sarah turned and ran over the knoll.

"Tell me how she is," Nellie shouted after her. "I'll help get her into the house."

Nellie hobbled over to the Sayers' front step and sat down. What if Sayers had killed his wife? And what if he woke up right away, in spite of what Sarah had said? Nellie's gaze shifted to where he lay on the ground.

It seemed as if Sarah had been gone for at least five minutes before Nellie finally saw her coming over the crest of the knoll with her mother. Mrs. Sayers was walking steadily, though she was leaning on her daughter's arm and her head was down.

As the two came to where Sayers was lying, Nellie was surprised to see them stop. She was even more astounded to see Mrs. Sayers put her arms under the man's shoulders and Sarah take his feet, to drag him across the grass and into the old shed attached to the log cabin. Nellie wondered why they even bothered.

In a few minutes, Sarah came back to Nellie with her mother. The girl's pale face was streaked with tear stains that Nellie had not noticed before.

"We're very sorry, Miss Mooney," said Mrs. Sayers. She was standing just behind Sarah and her face was turned down and to one side.

"I'm sorry, too," Nellie said. "I only wanted to ask about Sarah. I didn't want to cause any trouble."

"Oh, it wasn't your fault, Miss. It wasn't anyone's fault." Mrs. Sayers voice was trembling.

Nellie turned to look at her and gasped. "Ohhhh!" One side of the woman's face was a mass of bluish red. "Oh, Mrs. Sayers, you must see the doctor, you must."

"No, no!" Mrs. Sayers voice was stronger now. "I'll be fine. Tell me, did my husband hurt you? You were limping."

"No, that's just my ankle. I sprained that myself when I fell against the stoop inside the cowstable door."

"Here, take my arm," Mrs. Sayers offered. "We'll

help you inside. I'll bind up that ankle with some broadcloth. You'll find it a help till you get home."

"What about Mr. Sayers?"

"He won't move until tomorrow morning, at least."

"And then?"

"He won't remember anything."

"Maybe he should be told," Nellie said, as she stood on her good leg and tried to put a little weight on her injured foot. Mrs. Sayers put her right arm around Nellie's waist, and Nellie put her left arm around the small woman's shoulders. Sarah took Nellie's right hand, and together the three made their way to the shed attached to the cabin, and then in through the side-kitchen door.

The kitchen, the main room of the cabin, was small and dark and had only a single window, facing the driveway. A back door on the far side of the room opened into a small lean-to bedroom, and a ladder in the middle of the kitchen led up to a loft. A wooden cupboard stood against the wall nearest the stove, and beside it were a stool, a pail of water, and a basin. In front of the black stove lay a large, bright red, hooked mat — the only thing of beauty in the whole room, Nellie thought.

Mrs. Sayers led Nellie over to the dark brown horsehair couch that stood only a short distance from the front door. Sarah knelt in front of Nellie and undid her buttoned boot while Mrs. Sayers went to the cupboard drawer and fumbled around for some cloth.

The pain seemed to ease a little as Sarah pulled the boot off, but Nellie could see that her ankle was swelling. Mrs. Sayers came over to her and, with shaking hands, started to wrap the ankle firmly with wide strips of broadcloth. The left side of the woman's face was growing darker as though her wounds were bleeding inside.

"Mrs. Sayers, sit down beside me. I'll wrap my own ankle. You are shaking."

"I'm fine," the woman said again, but Nellie saw a slow tear trickle down the side of her cheek.

"Mrs. Sayers, sit down and rest."

Mrs. Sayers shook her head and kept binding Nellie's ankle.

"For Sarah's sake, see the doctor, and report your husband's behaviour."

Mrs. Sayers looked up at Nellie then. "Oh, Don has never touched Sarah. He would never lay a hand on Sarah."

"Why don't you just go away for a while? Take the money you planned for your trip at Christmas and go to see your folks now instead."

Mrs. Sayers looked surprised. "Our trip?"

"Yes. Sarah told me Mr. Sayers planned to keep enough from your harvest money to send you back to Ontario for a visit." Many a time that August as Nellie had come along the dusty road from Northfield School to the Mooney farm, she had seen the little girl and her mother dragging heavy sheaves of wheat as big as Sarah herself and stacking them together into large stooks. "Maybe if you're gone when he wakes up, he'll have some time to think about how he's been acting."

"Oh, he won't remember any of it, Miss. He never does."

"Maybe you should tell him."

"I have, but he doesn't believe me. He says I'm making it up to cause trouble and turn Sarah against him."

"But the bruises — doesn't he ask you about them?"

"He says I'm clumsy, always falling into doors. And sometimes I do, you know."

"Well, I'd have it out with him when he's sober . . . about the drinking."

"He says no woman's going to run his life and tell him what to do. He just gets so furious, he'll start to drink again and blame me for getting him riled. I try so hard, Miss Mooney, not to make him angry. But it just seems the least thing I say anymore gets him going."

"And if you say nothing, won't he drink anyway?"

"Yes, but sometimes it's a long time between his bouts. He may even go a couple of months. He didn't drink through most of the harvest."

"You had a good crop this year. So why don't you take Sarah and visit your parents back in Ontario? Sarah tells me she's never been to see them."

"We had a good garden too this year. I did preserves all summer. What with the strawberries and the saskatoons, it was a good crop. And we've loads of vegetables — potatoes, turnips, carrots, beets. We'll not go hungry this winter."

Mrs. Sayers stood up then and turned towards the cupboard to put back her supplies. Sarah was sitting on the floor beside Nellie with her head bent down. Looking at her more closely, Nellie could see that the child's shoulders were shaking and tears were streaming down her face.

"What's wrong, Sarah?" Nellie asked softly.

"We're not going to see Grandma and Grandpa after all — Pa spent all the money." The slight girl choked back her tears.

"He spent *all* the money?"

"All of it. And I can't have the new dress Ma promised me. I'm sorry, Miss Mooney, but I just can't go to school one more day in this old dress."

As Sarah broke into loud sobs, Mrs. Sayers turned and slipped quietly out of the room.

2

A splash of orange light from the setting sun fell across Nellie's shoulder as she leaned over to untie Bess, her chestnut mare.

"I'll be back soon, Sarah," she shouted, waving at the sad figure in the cabin doorway. Then she swung her small frame up into the saddle, noticing to her relief that the bandage on her ankle was making her foot stronger.

"Giddyup, Bess." Nellie slapped the reins lightly and the mare broke into a lively trot. Nellie knew she needed to hurry home, since it would soon be dark. Her own family farm was two miles to the northwest. A cold wind had picked up over the fields and was whipping the hair back from her face. A bank of slate-blue clouds was gathering in the west.

Nellie shivered as she remembered the bruise on Mrs. Sayers' cheek and the tears streaming down Sarah's face. All that suffering because of one man's drinking!

Nellie thought she had a good idea why Sayers drank. Manitoba could be a harsh and lonely place, and the lives of country people were filled with disappointments. Farmers spent long hours doing difficult work. They craved excitement and change. So a few drank.

"Well, Bess," Nellie said to her horse, "I'm going to have to do something about this. And I'll start by sewing a new dress for Sarah."

Nellie's planning was interrupted by the sound of a horse and buggy coming around the bend ahead. As the buggy came into full view, she recognized the Ingrams' majestic roan, and her heart sank.

The Ingrams lived on the farm just west of the Mooneys, and Mrs. Ingram had always hoped her son, Bob, would marry Nellie. The two *had* walked to Northfield School together every day when they were growing up. In Mrs. Ingram's mind, if not her husband, George's, it was simply a foregone conclusion that the children would marry some day. Things had not worked out that way, and Mrs. Ingram had still not quite forgiven Nellie.

Nellie could not understand her. After all, Bob had married five years before, in the summer of 1890, and was raising Clydesdale horses on a farm quite close to his parents' place. But Nellie was still not happy to meet Mrs. Ingram right on the edge of the Sayers' farm.

"Well, I see you've been visiting the Sayers," said Mrs. Ingram, drawing her roan to a halt. "It's a perfect scandal how that man drinks and keeps his wife and child in rags. But you won't be able to help. Goodness knows, I've tried!"

"You *have*?" Nellie's bright brown eyes opened even wider.

"Yes, I gave him a piece of my mind. Of course, I didn't get any thanks from the likes of him. And none from Eliza either. She just denies everything. So you might just as well stay away. Some people can't be helped." Mrs. Ingram looked down self-righteously, and her eyes fell upon Nellie's bound ankle. "What on earth has happened to you, Nellie?"

"Oh, nothing, really. I just twisted my ankle."

"Well, if you don't want to tell me what happened, I'll not be insulted. But I can guess. I hope you won't have to miss the lacrosse game between Wawanesa and Morden. My Bob's playing in that game tomorrow. I wouldn't miss it for the world."

"Oh, I'll be there, Mrs. Ingram. You can count on that! I'd never miss a game between Wawanesa and Morden!"

"Especially since the winner goes on to Winnipeg for the Western Canadian Championship. I can hardly wait!" With a firm flounce of the head, Mrs. Ingram gave her horse a slight touch with the reins, and she was off down the road.

Nellie sighed and flipped the reins a little to make Bess go faster. She simply had to go to that game, whether Mother wanted her to or not. Wes McClung was going to be playing on the

Wawanesa side, and this would be one of the last times she would see him before he went back east. He was leaving Monday morning.

Wes had finished his four years of apprenticeship at the drugstore in Manitou. Now he had only six months of courses left to complete his Phm.B. degree. But he had to take them at the University of Toronto. Then he would be able to work as a pharmacist back in Manitoba — unless he decided to stay in Ontario, of course. Nellie's heart sank at the thought.

Not that I really care, she reminded herself. Since she planned to devote her life to improving the lives of farm women, she might not have time for a husband. Still, if she were to get married, Wes would be the one. He was the only man she knew who truly believed in her. He even accepted her ideas about women getting the vote.

The sun had nearly disappeared behind the greyish-blue Brandon Hills northwest of the farm when Nellie turned into the lane. Pale fingers of light stretched between the bluffs of poplar, scrub oak, and hawthorne on the rolling land between the Hills and the house. But they were already beginning to shrink back, leaving pockets of darkness behind them.

The coal-oil lamp had been lit in the kitchen, casting a dim light onto the back stoop. Nellie turned away and steered her horse towards the barn.

Clang! Jack, Nellie's brother, had set his two milk pails on the path in front of her. Nellie had almost steered her horse right into him, but the intelligent animal had stopped just in time.

"Where do you think you're going? You're late, Nellie!" Jack snapped, sounding like his usual ornery self. Nap, the faithful old labrador, came up behind Jack, wagging his tail.

"I'm not that late, Jack Mooney, and don't get Mother started," Nellie shot back, her dark eyes flashing, as she swung down from the horse.

Jack's face broke into a wide grin. "Just teasing."

"Now I'm going to brush down Bess," Nellie said, ignoring the smile. "If Mother's upset, tell her, will you?"

"Hey! You face Mother with your own excuses. Don't pass the buck to me."

"I thought we were friends now, Jack! Be a dear and do what I say."

"Did I hear you say 'dear'? Are you in love or something?"

"No, just showing some sisterly affection."

"You mean you're trying to worm your way into getting *me* to suffer through Mother's lecture about *you* being late. I pity the poor man that marries you, Nellie Mooney. He'll have his hands full. I just hope he has the gift of the gab and a pocketful of smart retorts."

We're fighting again, Nellie thought. Only not as badly as when we were younger, thank goodness.

Since their father's death a few years before, Jack had softened a bit. And besides, there was less time for fighting, now that he had taken over the farm and Nellie was teaching in the Northfield School. She had come home to teach there this year, since Mother hadn't been well and had needed help with the housework.

"So how was life at Northfield today?" Jack said a bit apologetically.

"Oh, Sarah Sayers was away again, so I went to see her and —"

"What happened to your ankle? Playing soccer with the class again, eh, Nellie? Some of those senior boys are too strong for —"

"Yes, Jack Mooney, exactly right. And don't say a word of it to Mother."

"Yes, Your Highness. Umm, speaking of soccer and such things, do you still want to see the lacrosse game in Wawanesa tomorrow?"

"*Do* I? Wouldn't miss it for the world!"

"Thought not. Wes McClung playing, by any chance?"

"I don't know. Why do you ask?"

"Oh . . . no reason. Better get in for supper, Nell, Mother's probably waiting."

Nellie led Bess into the stable, smiling to herself. It didn't matter, she supposed, if Jack did know she was fond of Wes.

She groomed the horse, then headed back to the house. As she shut the back door and stepped into the clean-scrubbed light of the kitchen, she wondered what Mother thought of Wes. He and his sister had stopped by the farm twice that summer to take Nellie to the McClung's parsonage in Manitou for a visit. Wes hadn't come inside, and Mother had barely spoken to him. Still, she must have formed *some* impression. And as for what Wes thought of Nellie — she wasn't sure if he was really interested in her. Was she only a family friend, after all? She'd boarded with the McClungs for four years when she'd taught at Treherne and Manitou.

Nellie's thoughts were rudely interrupted.

"What kept you?" Mother said sharply, without even turning from the counter where she was cutting thick slices of bread from a fresh-baked loaf.

Well, Mother must be feeling better, Nellie thought as she threw her hooded hunter-green cloak over a hook on the back wall.

"I had extra lessons to prepare for Monday morning, Mother. It always takes longer on a Friday."

"But it's pitch-black outside. I'll have no woman from my household riding along the backroads, or any road for that matter, when there's not a speck of daylight in sight. Now check the potatoes, will you, please?"

Nellie slowly moved towards Mother's formidable black stove, trying to conceal her limp. If Mother noticed she was hurt, Nellie would have to sneak out to the lacrosse game behind her back.

Nellie picked up a fork to test the potatoes. She resented having to take orders from Mother again. She had lived away from home for five years — at Hazel, Manitou, and Treherne — and she'd loved her independence. Now she felt as if she were fourteen years old again.

"I am not a wee thing any more, Mother," Nellie protested. "I'm nearly twenty-two! I came and went as I pleased when I lived away from home, and no harm came of it."

"One day you'll go too far, though, Nellie. You need to learn caution."

"Yes, Mother. Many times I've heard you say that."

"And I believe your teaching career has made you just that much lippier. Watch your tongue, Nellie. It's unbecoming for a lady to speak her mind as much as you do."

"Hear, hear," said Jack from Father's rocking chair on the other side of the stove. "No man'll ever get a moment to propose, the way you go running on, Nellie." Jack lowered his copy of the *Scots Talisman* just enough for Nellie to see his eyes twinkling.

"You should be ashamed of yourself, Jack Mooney, playing the man of the house and reading the paper while Mother and I slave and sweat over the stove."

"Playing the man of the house? I *am* the man of the house, don't forget."

"You'll never replace —" Nellie stopped herself before she said, "Father." She missed him greatly — especially at moments like this. If he had still been with them, he would have interrupted the argument with a lighthearted comment and made her feel much better.

"Jack Mooney, you should visit the McClungs someday and see how a man should act in his home."

"Oh, it's the McClungs now, is it? Well, I wonder why that would be!"

"To teach you a lesson, that's why. The McClung boys washed up and helped with the cooking just the same as the girls."

"Stop your foolish talk, Nellie, and get to work.

Jack's been slaving out on the farm all day. Surely you don't expect him to work at night, too."

"Mother, I slaved —" Nellie stopped in mid-sentence. She knew there was no point in continuing. Letitia McCurdy Mooney was a stubborn, practical Scot, who believed a woman's job was to cook and clean and support her man's work. She would never think otherwise. Oh, to be back in Manitou. Nellie sighed.

"Nellie, you've been prodding the same potato ever since you arrived. Now, drain the water off, and help me take out the roast chicken."

As Nellie and her mother set the chicken on a large serving plate, Nellie bit her lower lip to keep back the tears. It had always been Father's job to take the bird out of the oven. Now she had to cooperate with Mother on yet another task — without Father to smooth things over.

"Come to the table now, Jack. We're ready."

Jack laid down the paper, ambled over to the head of the table, and sat down in what had always been Father's chair. Then he bowed his head and mumbled, "We thank Thee for this food. In Thy name, we pray. Amen. Now, please pass the potatoes."

"Carve the chicken first, Jack," Nellie said curtly.

"All right, you two," Mother said. "I thought we were finished with this quarrelling. We'll eat in silence if you cannot refrain from arguments."

Nellie fell silent, wishing again for Manitou and the refined conversation of the minister's table. At the McClungs there was always a topic of interest to be discussed: prohibition, women's votes, government policies. And when Mr. McClung was not present — George du Maurier's latest novel. But here there was only talk of the harvest and work. And there were long silences broken only by the ticking of the clock.

"Nellie, for the second time, *please* pass the carrots." Mother interrupted her thoughts. "I've never seen such a one as you to daydream. I hope it's not about some useless novel you've been reading."

"Thinking about the minister's son, I'll bet," Jack said, raising one eyebrow.

"Well," Nellie couldn't help smiling, "I was thinking how different life was when I was boarding at the McClungs'."

"And hoping you'd be boarding there again soon, and forever after?"

"I have no such lofty ambitions, Jack. Please pass the potatoes."

"I don't believe you. Hannah's found *her*self a Baptist minister and happily settled in Winnipeg. Now it's your turn. Hmm . . . a minister's son . . . Ministers do seem to be running in the family lately, eh, Mother?"

"I'm three years younger than Hannah, Jack. And I do not intend to settle down until I'm good and ready."

"Want to be an old maid, Nellie?"

"Carve me some chicken, will you please, Jack?" Mother interrupted.

"Yes, and I'd like a helping, too, if you can stop teasing me for a few minutes."

"Oh, Nellie L., I was just having some fun. I have to admit I missed you when you were away."

"You'll miss me a lot more if you keep on —"

"Nothing wrong with a good argument. But just to keep the family peace, I'll quit now. We can take things up again tomorrow on our way to the lacrosse game."

"Lacrosse game?" Mother said tersely.

The clock ticked loudly at the other end of the kitchen.

"Yes, the big one. The semifinal between Wawanesa and Morden. Wes McClung's playing."

Nellie cut into her chicken calmly, ignoring Jack's remark, hoping to upset him.

"And you're planning to go to this game, are you, Jack?"

"Yes. Everyone's going!"

"Well, you run the farm now, Jack. So I leave that to you. I know you'll make sure you're back in time for chores."

"Of course."

The clock kept ticking and Nellie kept quiet, hoping Jack would not say anything more about her going with him. There was no point in making an issue of it. She'd slip out with Jack after the noon meal.

"Too bad you might not be able to go after all, Nellie L. That game leg of yours."

Nellie went red with fury. So much for the truce with Jack. She pursed her lips and kept eating. Maybe Mother hadn't heard.

"What's that about a game leg? Nellie, whatever's the matter with your leg? I didn't know you had any trouble with your leg."

Nellie gave a sigh and began, "It's not my leg

exactly. It's my ankle. I twisted it today. You know how I like to play soccer with my pupils." She did not say she'd actually hurt her ankle playing soccer. So she really hadn't lied, she reasoned.

"Yes, I do know. And I can't understand it. You look too young to be teaching — then you act like a child, too. You worry me, Nellie, you really do. I don't think you'll ever grow up. Why, most women your age are married and have a couple of children by now."

Nellie was glad that Mother seemed to have forgotten about her ankle.

Then Jack said, "Well, Nellie L., my bet is you won't let it stop you from going to the game." He smiled craftily.

"Oh, no, Nellie will need to stay at home and let that foot heal up before Monday and school. You have responsibilities now that can't be taken lightly, don't you, Nellie? You can't just run off — like the time you were supposed to guard the cows in the pasture."

Nellie glared at Jack. "I'll be fine in the morning, Mother. I just twisted it a little." She couldn't help grimacing, though, as she stood up and started to help her mother clear the dishes from the table. Jack settled himself into Father's rocking chair beside the stove.

Mother glanced sharply at Nellie and said, "Well, Nellie L., I do think I should look at that ankle. Jack, give Nellie the rocking chair and pull up another chair for her leg."

Nellie smiled smugly at Jack as she sank into the coveted rocking chair and set her ankle on the chair Jack brought. Mother always did give the best of care to the sick and showed an understanding then that she did not often show at other times.

As Mother gently unwound the bandage from Nellie's swollen ankle, Nellie thought of her kindness. There wasn't a soul in the community who didn't have praise for Mrs. Mooney. She always came to the rescue when people were sick or injured.

"You have a bad sprain, young lady," her mother said, "but it's not broken." Nellie sighed with relief.

"However, it sometimes takes a sprain longer to heal than a clean break."

Mother *would* look on the grim side, Nellie thought. Well, no matter what, she was going to the game tomorrow, even if Jack had to carry her into the stands.

Mother rubbed Nellie's ankle with witch hazel and then wrapped it snugly again. "Now, don't you move off that chair, Nellie L. I'm off to your sister Lizzie's to help with a quilt. Your brother's driving me."

Now Nellie was very sorry about the sprained ankle. She would have loved to visit with Lizzie — her kind sister and confidante.

There was a bright side to this small disappointment, however. She could spend the rest of the evening reading without being pestered by Jack.

"Pass me that *Scots Talisman*, will you, Jack?" she said sweetly as her brother headed for the door. "And maybe that *Family Herald*, too."

Jack glowered as he handed the papers over to Nellie, knowing he was defeated.

"Be sure you rest now, Nellie," Mother repeated as she and Jack went out the door.

The latch clicked and Nellie burrowed into the *Family Herald*. Mother and Jack were not that bad, she told herself. But she could not understand why they opposed her in her dream of helping women. Wes supported her — and Father had always believed in her, too.

She could hear her father's kind voice saying, "I know you can do it, Nellie L. You'll help women just as you say you will."

It was Father who had first called her Nellie L. The L. stood for Letitia, her mother's name, but that wasn't the reason he called her that. He liked the musical sound the letter L made. Nellie took after her father that way, too, in the way she liked music.

She could hear his soft voice saying, "The Irish people have had so much trouble, they sing and dance and fight and laugh to keep their hearts from breaking."

"I'm glad you're Irish," Nellie had said. They were sitting on the bench outside the henhouse door, and she was watching her father sharpening his scythe. Nellie was almost ten.

"Well, you don't want to have a world full of singers and dancers, either, Nellie L.," Father went on. "Just think, if everyone sang and danced, no one would get any work done. Good thing we Irish can be full of fun and fond of music, yet serious, too, and earnest."

"I guess so," Nellie had sighed, "but now sing me the song about the red petticoat again." Nellie started to hum the old tune with its sad words and happy melody. And Father sang.

Shule, shule, shule, agra
It's time can only aise my woe
Since the lad o' me heart
From me did part
Shedate, avoureem, schlana
I'll dye my petticoat,
I'll dye it red
And through the world
I'll beg me bread . . .

Nellie smiled as she drifted off to sleep, remembering her Father's joyful ways. She would pass that joy on to all women who worked like slaves on farms and had no vote. Father would have been happy about that, and so would Wes.

3

"You've got more than the luck of the Irish, Nellie L.," Jack grumbled as he tapped his brown stallion, Barsac, with a whip. "It's a wonder Mother didn't keep you home."

It was three o'clock, the lacrosse game in Wawanesa had already started, and Jack and Nellie had only reached Millford. Jack touched Barsac's back lightly again, and the canopied buggy moved forward at a faster clip.

From between the buggy's open side curtains, Nellie gazed at the spot where Millford used to be. Goldenrod, wild sage, and Gaillardia bloomed on the site of the old mill, and a bracing September breeze sent prairie grasses rippling along like ocean waves.

"Are you listening to me or are you daydreaming again?" Jack grouched.

"What did you say?"

"See? You weren't listening!"

"Well, I am *now*, and you're not saying anything."

"I said I'm glad your ankle's better, so I won't have to cart you around! Also, it's too bad we're late."

"Cart me around! You are joking. As if I'd let you cart me around! And we're late 'cause you were delivering that calf. It's not my fault."

"I didn't say it was. Though now that you mention it, I did wait in the buggy for you to come out. And you did seem to be taking your time. But you look pretty good now."

Nellie turned and stared at her brother. He *was* changing. In the old days, arguments were just arguments. They never ended with compliments. Nellie glanced down at her red and grey wool skirt. It did look fetching with her hunter-green cloak and green felt hat. The only thing she didn't like about her outfit was her black goatskin shoes. They were peeled and gaping a bit at the top, and her ankle bandage was spilling over the sides of the right one. Nellie wished she'd had the foresight to move the buttons over the night before, instead of falling asleep.

"You don't look too bad yourself," Nellie conceded.

"Thank you, Nellie L. Now hang on to your hat. I'm going to let Barsac go faster. The game may be half over already and we have two miles yet to go. Giddap, Barsac."

Ten minutes later, the horse and shiny black buggy pulled into the Wawanesa fairgrounds, then drew to a sudden halt at the stables behind the grandstands. At that moment, the puffy white clouds that had been covering the sun all morning moved on, and the grounds were flooded with the brilliant light of a September afternoon. Shouts from the spectators rose into the frosty air, then faded away into the sand hills of the Assiniboine to the north.

"You go ahead, Nell. I'll find my own spot in the grandstand after I get this horse into the stable."

"Thanks, Jack, I'll see you after the game." Nellie began running towards the grandstands, but immediately slowed down. Her ankle was not in as good shape as she had led Mother to believe.

Nellie clambered up into the second row of seats, just behind the Wawanesa players' bench. As she was settling in, she spotted Mr. and Mrs. Ingram to her left, on the seat behind her. The Burnetts, whose farm was just southwest of the Mooneys', were sitting just behind the Ingrams. Nellie did not recognize the older man on her right side. The couple on her left were also strangers to her. They had two children with them: a freckle-faced boy of about ten, and a girl not much older. Probably from Morden, she decided.

Nellie leaned over towards the grey-haired gentleman beside her. "Who's winning?"

"Well, our Morden boys are showing the Wawanesa lads a thing or two about Canada's national sport. The score's six to five and we're almost through the third quarter."

"Six to five!" Nellie groaned in dismay.

"Yup, our boys might just as well pack their bags now for the finals in Winnipeg."

Whack! Something had fallen on the man's shoulder. Looking up, Nellie saw that it was an umbrella — one she recognized. It was Mrs. Ingram's flowered one. Could she actually have hit the poor man?

"I'll give you to understand that my Bob's just getting warmed up!"

The man looked up in silent astonishment.

"Tut, tut." Mrs. Ingram clicked her tongue and waved one finger back and forth. "Such bad form — counting the score before the game is over!"

Just then a stout woman, probably the Morden man's wife, stood up and swung her heavy canvas lunchbag at Mrs. Ingram. But Mrs. Ingram ducked, and the lunchbag flew into Mr. Burnett's lap.

"Thanks for the lunch, Ma'am." Mr. Burnett smiled with his usual good humour. He set the bag down beside him, took out an apple, then tossed the bag back to the enraged lady.

"How dare you?" she shouted at Mrs. Ingram, while the two children on Nellie's left started to shout, "Hurray for Morden! Three cheers for the red and yellow!"

At that moment, a few of the players on the Wawanesa bench turned around to see what was causing all the ruckus. Among them was Wes — Nellie had spotted the number eight on his white and blue striped shirt — and now their eyes met.

They were only a short distance apart. Nellie smiled widely and waved her hand high in the air. But Wes just nodded his head and turned back to the game.

Just then the coach leaned over and tapped Wes on the back, and he trotted onto the field while the players cheered. The elbows of Wes's shirt were patched — a sure sign that he was not afraid of rough play. Some dried blood was also smeared on the left shoulder of his sweater.

The field showed the telltale marks of a summer's worth of lacrosse games. The areas around both the nets, and the middle sections of the field were completely bare of grass. Since it had rained so little that autumn, these patches were as hard and dusty as a well-packed dirt road. Any player who fell there would really feel it.

Wes nodded to Bob Ingram as Ingram left the field. The referee's whistle cut through the tension in the air. It was the end of the third quarter, and the teams were changing direction. Nellie realized with some satisfaction that the Morden goalie would now have to squint into the setting sun. Perhaps Wawanesa's luck would change.

"You look worried, Nellie L.," said Mr. Burnett between bites of his newly acquired apple.

"The score *is* six to five — and not in our favour!"

"No need to be too concerned," Mr. Burnett replied. Nellie liked his reassuring tone. It reminded her of how good she'd felt when Mr. Burnett let her enter the race at the Millford picnic when she was a young girl — even though the competition had only been open to boys.

"But we're losing!" Mr. Ingram interrupted.

"Yes, but did you notice Wawanesa's change in strategy at the beginning of the second quarter?"

"The bounce shots, you mean?" Nellie asked.

"Yes, the first two Wawanesa goals in the second quarter were scored on bounce shots."

"Yeah, the boys from Morden did start to look a bit worried then."

"And Wawanesa scored three more goals during the third quarter."

"Guess you're right, Burnett. The tide might be turning," Mr. Ingram said doubtfully.

"Did you see that young Wes McClung, Ingram?"

"Did I! He's the best on the team."

"Now, just a minute, George," Mrs. Ingram interrupted her husband. "I wouldn't go that far. Our Bob is doing an excellent job!"

"Yes, Nancy," Mr. Burnett answered, "but I'll wager the change in strategy was Wes's idea. He spent an awfully long time jawing with the coach and the players at the half-time break."

Nellie looked proudly at Wes. So *you're* the secret of our success, she thought.

At the beginning of the fourth quarter, Wes crouched down to take the faceoff. The referee placed the ball between the back of the two players' sticks. The whistle blew. Wes drew his stick back faster than the opposing centreman did. Then scooping the ball up, he threw it to Elick King. Farther down the field, Wawanesa's Stuart Humphreys was waiting to take the pass from Elick.

The ball never reached Humphreys. Morden's

goaltender, John Cameron, frustrated by Wawanesa's bounce shots, decided to take matters into his own hands. Before King made his pass, Cameron used the twenty feet between him and Humphreys to gather up some speed. As Humphreys turned to receive the pass, he was levelled by a freight train named Cameron.

Humphreys lay on the ground, motionless. The Morden players congratulated Cameron, but the Wawanesa players cried foul. The referee warned both teams about hitting from behind but ruled this one a legal side-hit. Humphreys was cheered as he limped groggily off the field. Another cheer went up as Bob Ingram re-entered the game.

"You show 'em, Bob," Mrs. Ingram shouted twice. She didn't seem to mind that she was the only one still cheering.

Wes had possession of the ball. And every player and fan knew what a missed pass could mean. Morden was famous for being able to hang onto the ball and waste time so that the other side got no second chances at possession.

Bob and Wes might save the day: they were two of Wawanesa's top players. But both played with such intensity that they often wore themselves right out. Wes had been running and jostling for the ball for a good part of the game. But Wes then had to endure many pokes and hits from the opposing team. This rough play had taken its toll.

The Wawanesa team really had only one major advantage: the setting sun behind the Wawanesa net was becoming an obstacle to the Morden players.

Now, Wes and Bob were bearing down on the

Morden net.

Bob had the ball and there was only one Morden player left to cover him and Wes. That player darted over to check Bob, but it was too late. Bob had already thrown the ball over the opposing player's head and into Wes's stick.

With nobody between him and the goalie, Wes raced towards the goal. He unleashed a blistering bounce shot that for the sixth time that afternoon passed the goaltender and slammed into the net!

The Morden goalie dug the ball out of the net and hurled it at the throng of cheering Wawanesa players gathering around Wes. The ball hit Wes in the back of the head.

"Hey, who threw that!" Bob yelled. The referee blew his whistle and all action on the field stopped. In the stands, murmurs went up.

"I think my Bob's been hurt," Mrs. Ingram screamed, jumping to her feet and dropping her umbrella on the ill-fated man from Morden.

"Take it easy, dear," her husband said. "Someone got hit on the head — but I think it's the McClung boy."

Yes, it's Wes, Nellie said to herself as she saw him stand up and rub the back of his head.

"Never again, McClung!" yelled the Morden goalie.

"Add one minute for injury time," barked the referee to the timekeeper. Wes walked briskly to the bench and waved at the people in the stands.

Is he waving at me or at everybody? Nellie wondered. It was difficult to tell. But one thing was sure: he was hardly injured at all. No cold compresses came out. Wes wasn't even sitting on the bench. He was in a huddle with the rest of the Wawanesa team. The score was tied now, and the air was buzzing with suspense.

In seconds, both teams had returned to the field. Last faceoff, Nellie thought, then noticed her fingers were aching. She'd been gripping the edge of the bench since Wes had been blindsided.

"All right, lads, this has been a good, clean match. Let's keep it that way. Not much time left in the game now." Then the referee blew the whistle.

Morden won the faceoff and had the ball down at the Wawanesa end in no time. Suddenly a Morden player made a pass from behind the Wawanesa net to a teammate racing in front of the Wawanesa goalie. But Elick King surprised everyone by intercepting the pass and throwing the ball to mid-field. A cloud of dust went up as a pair of Wawanesa players and two Morden boys fought for the ball.

"There can't be more than one minute left in the game," said the man from Morden.

"Plenty of time for Wes to get another goal," Nellie said abruptly.

From the dust cloud emerged the blue and white stripes of a Wawanesa player. Wes McClung had prevailed! As he pulled his stick back for the long throw to an unguarded Bob Ingram, the Morden goalie began charging the unsuspecting Bob. Wes faked the pass and Bob ducked the hit. A great "aah" rose from the crowd as they realized what had happened. Wes had thrown the ball not at Bob but into a yawning net!

"Peee-eep!" The referee's whistle pierced the Wawanesa cheers. "That's the game!" he yelled.

The scorekeeper, oblivious to the noise, methodically registered the final goal on the scoreboard. Another cheer went up when the number 7 card was finally hung on its hook under the words Home Team.

Nellie leapt to her feet faster than Mrs. Ingram ever had. "Wes McClung! You did it! You did it! You won the game!" She grabbed her umbrella and started to beat the seat in front of her.

"Excuse me, sir, I don't know your name," she said to the man from Morden, "but isn't that number eight the best player you've ever seen?"

"Can't say I share your enthusiasm, Miss," he mumbled, but Nellie did not notice.

"Wes, you're the best!"

Nellie was catching her breath before launching into her next series of shouts and yelps when she felt something tapping her shoulder. It was Mrs. Ingram's umbrella again.

Nellie turned around and looked up to see Mrs. Ingram staring at her, open-mouthed. Then she noticed that Mr. Burnett was also examining her with interest — and smiling broadly.

Nellie's face turned beet red. She'd be the talk of the town tomorrow. Letitia Mooney's daughter throwing herself at the McClung boy. Oh, well, she consoled herself, what did it matter? Wes *was* the best player on the team!

Pushing all thoughts of Mrs. Ingram out of her mind, Nellie jumped down from the grandstand and walked over to the side of the playing field.

She hardly noticed her ankle anymore and had completely forgotten about her goatskin shoes. Her heart swelled with pride as she saw Wes break away from the rest of his teammates and stride across the field towards her.

"So what do you think, Nellie Mooney?"

"I think you're the best lacrosse player this side of Lake Superior — and probably in the whole country!"

Wes looked down at his feet, then back at Nellie. There was a half-grin on his face and a twinkle in his eye. "Yeah, not bad, eh? The team played well."

"Oh, Wes, why don't you give yourself some credit? You were the best and that's all there is to it!"

"If you think so, Nellie L."

"I know so — and so does everybody for miles around!"

"I'll sure miss going to Winnipeg for the finals." His tousled red hair was clumped in sweat. The breeze was beginning to cool his hot cheeks but the perspiration continued to drip from his chin. His deep blue eyes, however, were as serene as they always were.

"Yes . . . it's . . ." Nellie had forgotten what she meant to say.

Mr. Burnett came up to Wes and was slapping him on the shoulder. "Wes McClung, I don't know if I've ever watched a better lacrosse game. You're a real inspiration. My grandson just told me he can't wait to get his own stick and start practising with some school chums. He says he wants to wear your number eight when you retire. You and the rest of the lads did us proud."

"It was a lot of fun. A great day for lacrosse in Wawanesa!"

"Better than playing cards, eh?" Mr. Burnett grinned at Wes, gave him another slap on the shoulder, and moved off. Nellie noticed the smile leave Wes's face.

"You getting ribbed about playing cards again, Wes?" Nellie asked. She remembered people in Manitou teasing Wes for enjoying a game of cards.

"Yes, once a minister's son, always a minister's son. I find it annoying at times."

"Hey, Wes! C'mon!" Stuart Humphreys and Elick King had come up behind Wes and Nellie on their way to the dressing room.

"I'm coming," Wes shouted. "See you later, Nellie. Maybe at supper." Then he turned and raced away to join his celebrating teammates.

Nellie watched him go, then started to scan the crowd to find her brother. She knew he planned to stay for the celebration supper in the yard of the Wawanesa Methodist Church. As Nellie looked around, her eyes fell on Tom Simpson, the blonde-haired man who worked in the drygoods store. He was always stopping to chat with her when they met on the street. He wasn't bad looking either. More than one fish in the sea, Nellie thought. Wes McClung might have some competition there.

4

An hour later, Nellie stepped carefully down the front steps of the Methodist parsonage, holding two thick lemon pies with high white topping, lightly browned — to perfection. She was taking them next door to the church yard, where tables had been set and women were serving both Morden and Wawanesa guests.

"Those pies look great, Nellie. Did you bake them?" Wes said as he caught up to her.

"No, not me! My mother did." Nellie smiled. "Have you eaten yet?"

"I ate with the fellows, but I can always handle another piece of pie."

"Just follow me, Wes McClung. I'll see you get a piece. Mother's lemon pie is unbeatable."

There were a few spaces still at the end of the table, so Nellie led Wes over there, where they weren't too close to the rest of the crowd.

"So you still get teased about being a minister's son," she said, beginning where their conversation had left off.

"I try not to let it bother me. But sometimes it does."

"Why? Surely not the part about playing cards?"

"Lots of people think it's not right. And maybe it isn't. I don't gamble, though."

"Wes, I think I hear your father in you. And you know he can be far too stern."

"Not always. He knows how to have a good time, too."

"Sometimes. But he puts so much energy into his work for the church, there's not much left to have fun with."

"Yes, I seem to have a lot more fun than he does!" Wes gave Nellie a big smile, and she knew he was thinking about the lacrosse game.

"And you should keep having fun. You're a super athlete, Wes, everyone loves you, and you're clever at cards. It would be a crime to waste those talents!"

"But maybe I'm not doing my duty. I should probably work as hard as Father does."

"But we're meant to use our talents. That's your duty, too!"

"You've got me there, Nellie. As you usually do. You're one of the cleverest women I know."

"Did I hear you correctly, Wes McClung?" It was

Jack. He *would* happen to be strolling by, just as things were getting interesting, Nellie grumbled to herself.

"Oh, hello, Jack. How'd you like the game? Great to beat Morden, eh?"

"Yes, it was. And great playing, Wes. But did I overhear you telling my sister she was clever?"

"Yes, I'm proud to say you did."

"What lies have you been telling him now, Nellie?" Jack grinned.

"I just won a little argument fair and square, according to the rules of debate."

"Rules of debate!" Jack snorted. "You mean you nattered at him till he gave up."

"Jack, you know that's not true."

"Oh, yes, it's true. And you're going to keep nagging at men until they give women the vote."

"Just the way *men* would nag women if men didn't have the vote!"

Jack's face went red but Wes looked at Nellie with admiration.

"Another point for Nellie, I'm afraid, Jack."

"Oh, don't tell me she's convinced you, too. There'll never be an end to it."

"She doesn't need to convince me. I support her completely."

"You do? Oh, well, let's change the subject. I want to introduce you to Barbara Wilkie."

For the first time, Nellie noticed that one of the Wilkie girls was standing beside her brother. Jack didn't need to introduce her. Everyone knew the Wilkie girls from Treesbank about a mile north of Wawanesa. Jack must be a bit flustered.

Barbara Wilkie smiled and said, "Hello, Nellie and Wes."

Barbara was a pretty girl, Nellie thought. Younger than Jack, she had thick, dark brown hair that hung almost to her waist.

"So you're not going to Winnipeg, Wes," Jack said.

"No, I'm leaving for Toronto."

"I envy you."

"You envy me?"

"Yes, I should have stayed in school, but it's a bit late now. I wanted the farm life, and now that Father's gone I have no choice anyway."

"That's not so bad, is it?"

"Maybe not. I can't say I don't like it. Just lately, I've started training standardbred horses. Someday I'll have the fastest trotter in Western Canada."

Nellie couldn't help smiling. Jack always liked to brag and now, in front of Barbara, he was even worse than usual. But he had certainly succeeded in getting the girl's attention. Her soft brown eyes opened wide as Jack talked about his stallions.

"Well, I'll probably be mixing medicines for your trotters when I get back west."

"I'll call on no one else. But in the meantime, I want to drive Barbara home. And I'll be back, Nellie, to get you by five o'clock."

"Oh, don't worry yourself, Jack," Wes interrupted. "I'll drive Nellie home."

"I don't know about that," Jack replied. "Mother's orders, you know. I'm to make sure Nellie gets home safe and sound."

"I'll make sure she does," Wes smiled.

"That would be just wonderful, Wes," Nellie said, taking matters into her own hands. "You see, Mother thinks Jack has much more wisdom and foresight than I do. Part of her Old World reverence for men, I believe. So it's Jack's job to make sure I don't get into scrapes — even though I've been fending for myself for five years."

"You never miss a chance, do you, Nellie!" Jack grinned. "Well, I'm just as happy to spend more time with Barbara, so I'll leave it that way. Mind you, McClung, if Nellie isn't home by eight, you'll hear from me . . ."

"Right, Mooney. We'll be on time." Wes winked at Nellie as Jack and Barbara strolled past the grandstand to the stables. "Now, Nellie, we have the rest of the day to ourselves. And I've been looking forward to it."

"Me, too, Wes. After Monday, I won't be seeing you for a long time." Although Wes and Nellie had known each other for almost five years — even before he took his first months of pharmacy training — they hadn't actually spent much time alone together.

Nellie took Wes's arm, and he looked down at her with some concern. "I meant to tell you before, but I'm leaving tomorrow. I'm supposed to register at U. of T. on Tuesday, and the train trip alone takes two days."

"Tomorrow?" Nellie tried to sound indifferent. After all, Wes was nothing more than a good friend.

****

It was five o'clock, and Wes and Nellie were walking through the fields outside Wawanesa. They had spent the last hour chatting with folks in the yard of the Wawanesa Methodist Church. When they'd tried just talking to each other there, it seemed they were always being interrupted — by teammates and wellwishers who had heard that Wes was leaving for Toronto.

"Are you limping?" Wes asked, looking down at the black goatskin shoes that, so far, Nellie had successfully concealed.

"I might as well admit it. I've been trying to hide it from you all day."

"What happened, Nellie? Not another fall off your horse, I hope."

"No . . . It was . . . Promise not to tell anyone, Wes?"

"Of course, I promise."

"You know little Sarah Sayers? I went to visit her yesterday, since she was missing school. And her father —"

"Nellie, that drunken Sayers? Did he lay a hand on you?"

"No, no. But he did . . . lunge for me in a drunken state. I fell against a stone stoop and sprained my ankle."

"And you've been limping around all day? Now, sit down over there," Wes said, pointing to an old granite rock surrounded by clumps of goldenrod. "You need to stay off that foot."

"Oh, you are a worrier, Wes," Nellie said. But her ankle really was getting sore, so she took Wes's advice and headed over to the rock.

"That Sayers," Wes said with disgust. "The way he's treated his wife and daughter over the years . . . It makes me wonder what God is doing. Doesn't He see all their suffering?"

"I believe He sees."

"Well, He must take pleasure in it, then. Otherwise, He would stop it."

"No, He respects us too much for that."

"What do you mean?"

"Well, Mr. Sayers is suffering too. And God is giving him a chance to take matters into his own hands and do the right thing by his wife and daughter."

"Sayers? God cares a fig for Sayers? That man is a fiend. He deserves what's coming to him."

"Wes McClung, how can you say such a thing? You're sounding like your father again. Black and white. Right or wrong."

"And if Sayers does not turn around? What then?"

"God will judge him with mercy . . . I think. Only He knows a person's heart."

"God might not be so easy on him."

"Then it should be God who judges, not us. Wes, I have the greatest respect for your father and his devotion to the Methodist Church. But I wish he had not passed on such dramatic views of eternal punishment."

Wes smiled a little at her remarks. "Well, I hope what you say is true, but . . ."

"No buts, Wes. You have such a fine conscience. You can always find all sorts of reasons to punish yourself — and others. But I think it's the way you were brought up more than who God really is."

"Well, I guess I am a bit of a beggar for punishment. I'm heading out to Toronto tomorrow, and even before I get there, I'll already be behind in my reading."

A flock of geese flew overhead, honking as they went.

"Sounds like keening, Wes, doesn't it?" Nellie said.

"Keening?"

"Yes, the mourning songs of the Irish."

"Ah, yes, perhaps."

"Will you be snowed under all term, Wes?"

"Yes, Nellie. I may be too busy to write much. I hope you'll understand . . ."

Nellie gulped. Was this Wes's way of telling her their correspondence was over? Perhaps he could hardly wait to go. In her mind's eye, Nellie saw a circle of beautiful Toronto girls wearing well-cut clothes and engaging in important conversations with Wes. She was just a country girl. What chance had she against their sophistication and knowledge?

"Nellie, you haven't answered my question. Will you understand and write just the same, even if I can't?"

"Of course I'll write," she answered, her hopes rising, "but I will miss your letters if you can't find time to . . ."

"Oh, I'll try, all right. And I'm going to give you something to keep you thinking of me when I'm gone."

"Give me something?" Nellie barely had time to

get the words out before she saw what Wes meant. He pulled a little black box out of his pocket and flipped back the lid.

"An opal! Wes, do you know that's my birthstone?"

"Of course, Miss Mooney. That's why I chose it." His eyes shone more brightly than the ring, and his voice softened. "I won't be here for your birthday, Nell, but I don't want you to forget I'll be thinking of you."

Nellie took the little ring from its box and put it on the third finger of her right hand.

"Oh, Wes, how thoughtful of you." Nellie threw her arms around his neck and just as quickly removed them.

But Wes reached over and put his left arm around Nellie's shoulders. Then he took her right hand in his free one and stroked the ring on her third finger. "Nellie, do you remember our promise to tell each other . . . if there was ever anyone else?"

"Yes."

"And do you remember we promised to be friends forever . . . no matter what?"

"I remember."

"Well, there is no one else for me. I haven't met anyone I like to be with as much as I like to be with you."

Nellie looked up and saw another flock of geese flying south.

"Nellie," Wes said, hesitating, "is there anyone else for you?"

"No, Wes, there isn't. And I don't know whether there ever will be."

"So I hope you'll continue to write to me," Wes smiled. "And if we meet someone else, we'll tell each other right away?"

"Yes, and we'll always be friends, Wes." Nellie looked down at the ring, then up again at the rapidly fading sun. "But, really, I'm so busy I doubt I'll meet anyone new back on the farm. But you . . . you . . ."

"Oh, I'd tell you, Nellie. And I'm going to be busier than you. I'll have too much work to do to make new friends. Anyway, I think I'll always like the old ones best. And, Nellie, I understand about your wanting to help women. I'd never stand in your way. You know that, don't you?"

"Yes, Wes, I know. That's one reason we'll always be friends." Nellie smiled at Wes, and he gave her hand a squeeze. "And I'd like to sit here with you forever, but . . ."

"But I've got to get you back before eight or there'll be Jack to answer to!"

"Yes, and I just bet you haven't packed a thing, Wes McClung, so you'd better get going. Your mother won't make your sister do it for you. She's not like my mother."

Wes laughed and pulled Nellie up from the rock. As they started back to the livery stables, a third flock of geese flew above them, keening — or singing of adventure. Nellie was not sure which.

5

"Whoa, Bess," Nellie said. Her chestnut mare was trotting past the entrance to the Northfield School and on towards the open field. "Do you think we're going for a run today?"

Bess snorted but let Nellie guide her towards the lone Manitoba maple at the corner of the school. It was now mid-October, and a layer of snow covered the fields that stretched away in every direction. To the north were the sandhills of the Assiniboine and to the west was Oak Creek, bordered by a belt of elm and spruce.

The night before, the temperature had taken a sudden drop, but in spite of the cold, the air was bright and clear. Bess's coat shone under the sun's rays like burnished oak.

As Nellie tied Bess to the hitching post in the

school shed, she thought back to the very first day she had come here. The school had been new then and smelled of freshly cut wood, and she had been a pupil. Now, twelve years later, she was the teacher.

Inside, the desk at the front of the room had been painted dark brown to cover the scratches and scrapes of long service, and the walls had become smoked from twelve years of fires. A square box stove sat on four short, chubby legs in the middle of the room, like a big black bear cub. It was surrounded by a tin fence decorated with the dripping mittens of one or two pupils who had already arrived.

Nellie draped her own mittens on the fence, hung her coat on a peg on the west wall, and started writing the morning's lessons on the board. She hoped the day would go by quickly, since she'd just received her first letter from Wes. She would not have time to read it properly until school was over.

"Miss Mooney, Miss Mooney," Nellie heard a little voice say.

"Yes, Annabelle, what is it?"

"I seen you at the drygoods store on Saturday. Why was you talking to Tom Simpson?"

"Oh, I was . . . thinking about buying material for a new dress."

"They've got some awful nice pieces of cloth."

"Yes, they have."

"Miss Mooney, you still got that limp. How did you hurt yourself?"

"Oh, I sprained it a while ago. It's a bad sprain, but don't worry about it. It'll be better soon."

****

By nine o'clock, most of the pupils were in their seats, leaning forward on their desks. The steamy smell of wet woollens filled the air.

Through one of the three side windows, Nellie could see two boys running past the lone Manitoba maple. They were Senior Fourths who were often late because they had to help with morning chores at home. Nellie heard them stomp the snow from their feet as they reached the outer porch.

"Hurry to your desks, boys," she said as they entered. "Now, class, we will sing the national anthem."

Twenty squeaky voices launched into "God Save the Queen."

"Now I would like you to open your readers to today's lessons."

Two older girls from the Senior Fourth class were sitting in the back two corners of the one-room schoolhouse listening to children from Junior First. Another girl from the same senior class was sitting on the low platform at the front, right behind the teacher's desk, reading to the young primer class. These helpers had already completed their own senior reading lessons with Nellie and hoped to be teachers some day.

On the far left of the platform, little Johnny Newell was swinging his crossed left leg back and forth and smirking as though it were an honour to sit there. He'd been caught flipping a spitball towards Sarah Sayers. Nellie knew he was desperately trying to get the girl's attention, but Sarah didn't know that, and tears had welled up in her eyes as the spitball stung into the right side of her face. Sarah never seemed far from tears these days, and Nellie couldn't help wondering what was happening at home. The girl was still wearing the same shabby dress and shoes.

Nellie walked to the back of the room and leaned over to help the two latecomers. They had just returned to school, for they had been busy until now helping at home with the harvest.

As she listened to them read, her eyes scanned the classroom. Someone in the senior class was missing: Betty Jones, again. Nellie realized that the girl had been absent for a week now. That was unusual, Nellie thought. Betty was an eager student and hardly ever missed a day.

When the boys had finished their reading, Nellie called the senior girls back to their seats. "Now we'll go over the new arithmetic lesson." She worked through the new sums on the front blackboard. The classes were going like clockwork. After five years of experience, Nellie was skilled at managing nine different levels at once.

"There's your homework for tonight," she said when she'd finished the lesson. She pointed to the right side of the front blackboard. "You may work on those problems now while I work with the Junior Third class."

Pencils clacked, and every head in the Senior Fourth bent over a desk, for each knew that every bit of work done now would save time later.

Before beginning the Junior Third's lesson, Nellie stopped to speak to Annabelle Gable, who sat at the front of the right side aisle. "Betty has been away for a week now. Do you know if she's sick?" Annabelle did not look up, but everyone else in the Senior class did.

"You wouldn't mind taking work home to her, would you?" The Gables lived on the farm next to the Jones'. "I don't like to see Betty fall too far behind."

"I don't know, Miss Mooney," Annabelle mumbled. "My parents . . . Anyway, I can't take her work over."

"Why not?" Nellie asked, staring at her student with puzzled eyes.

"'Cause Ma won't let me near her," Annabelle said, still looking down at her slate.

"What on earth has she caught? Smallpox?" Nellie was alarmed.

"I don't know, Miss Mooney," said Annabelle. "Ma won't say. Just says I'm to keep away from there or she'll tan me good."

Nellie stared at Annabelle's blonde curls, then gazed around at the other senior pupils, who were all looking up at her. Two of the girls caught each other's eye and giggled. One boy smirked at them before he turned back to his sums.

Nellie gasped. Surely Betty was not . . . The thought crossed her mind and left again. Surely not, she decided. But whatever was causing this strange reaction from the students, she knew she should not pursue it further at this time.

"Well, back to work everyone. Remember, I'll be checking your homework first thing in the morning."

Nellie's thoughts lingered on Betty. She would drop by the Jones' place herself this evening and take along the schoolwork. She would be welcomed, she knew, for Betty's parents, though older than most, were very caring. Betty was their only child. Some said that the Jones' made their daughter work too hard on the farm, but there was no one else at home to help them.

Nellie remembered the day Betty had told her she wanted to be a nurse. She was a bright girl, so Nellie had persuaded her parents to let her spend more time on her schoolwork. They had recently taken on hired help, and this fall Betty had been able to attend school regularly. Nellie had been encouraged by her progress and thought she should try her final exams that June. She still had a year and a half of work to cover. But with hard work, Nellie thought she could do it.

But recently, Nellie had become somewhat uneasy about Betty. More than once lately, she had noticed a man with a fine horse and buggy picking her up on Sundays after church. And the buggy did not go in the direction of the Jones' farm. It drove towards Wawanesa.

The man who drove the gleaming chestnut mare was the assistant bartender at Charlie's Place, the local bar. He was such a soft-spoken man that Betty's parents probably knew nothing of his bad reputation. Besides, they trusted their lovely daughter. Nellie cringed a little at her own thoughts. She hoped she was wrong and that her pupils were only reacting to their parents' gossip. There was bound to be gossip about a girl who was seen with John.

A hand was waving in a semicircle to Nellie's right.

"Yes?" Nellie mumbled absently to eleven-year-old Jane Weber in the Senior Second class. Jane was small for her years but made up for her size with sheer loudness.

"Ma says she heard the inspector is coming. Our cousin came over from Treesbank last week and she said he'd been there. Wednesday to Friday that was. Everybody knows his route, Ma says. This week, he's at Wawanesa."

"Thank you for telling me that."

"But, Miss Mooney, I'm not finished yet. He'll probably be at Wawanesa all week. Their school has three rooms, you know. But then he'll be here bright and early Monday morning. Ma said you'd want to know, Miss Mooney."

"Thank you, Jane, that's nice of your mother to tell me — but when he comes, we'll just continue our lessons as usual. Now, open your readers, everyone in Senior Second class, at page nineteen, and be prepared to read at any time. Peter, you may begin reading 'The Hare with Many Friends.'"

As Peter began, Isabel, a little girl who was usually very shy, put her hand up and waved even more frantically than Jane had.

"Just a minute, Peter," Nellie said. "Yes, Jane?"

"Miss Mooney, I think I should tell you . . ." she said with considerable hesitation. Nellie's breath caught a little. She knew now that the question would not be a comfortable one.

"Yes, Isabel, what is it?" Nellie said kindly.

"Well, Pa says he heard Mrs. Dale tell Mr. Burnett

that he ought to tell the inspector about your views on women voting. But Mr. Burnett said he'd not say one word to the inspector, him being a friend of your ma and brother. But he sure was going to speak to you about it."

Mrs. Dale was an overworked farm woman whom Nellie had first met at the Millford picnic over ten years ago. Her husband was prosperous now, but the poor woman was still overworked, with six children and another on the way. Four of them were sitting right there in Nellie's classroom. Nellie was surprised the woman even had time to gossip!

All eyes turned now towards the oldest Dale boy, who was still in the Senior Third class. He'd fallen a class behind, since he'd been absent so much. He quietly hung his head and studied his inkwell.

Nellie's eyes opened wider as the shy Isabel continued. "And Mrs. Ingram says she can't blame Mrs. Dale for speaking her mind. But she said she won't say anything herself on account of your mother being her best friend."

"Isabel, I think we should get back to our lessons." Nellie looked down at her reader.

"I think you should know, Miss, that since your mother isn't so sick anymore, Mrs. Ingram's going over to tell her what you've been up to — teaching your students that women should have the vote. I'm sorry, Miss Mooney. But Ma says you should know what folks are saying."

"Someday, women *will* have the vote! I believe that!" Flushed a bit, Nellie stared back at Isabel. "Now, we will proceed with the lesson."

Nellie's cheeks were flaming as she thought of those old friends of the family. How could Mrs. Ingram and Mr. Burnett talk that way about her? She'd just ask them the very next time they met.

****

At four o'clock, the busy day ended for the students, and as usual, they all tore outside. Nellie never had managed an orderly dismissal. But the younger ones always followed on the heels of the older ones, and no one was ever hurt. One secret of successful teaching, Nellie had found, was not to fix what was already working.

Nellie cleaned the boards and wrote out the lessons for the next day. Then she pulled on her hunter-green cloak and stepped outside. At last, she would be able to read the letter from Wes.

To her surprise, the day's snow had completely melted. The sun was still beaming brightly, and the air was even warm. Nellie took off her cloak, threw it over her arm, and headed towards the school shed. She had a secret in there. It was a hammock that she often slung between the shed and the Manitoba maple after school when the weather was warm enough.

This will be my last chance to lie in the hammock till next spring, Nellie thought. I'd better take advantage of it. It was the one time of day when Nellie could just let her mind drift. From the moment she walked in the door at home, Mother would keep her so busy she could barely think. Then, after the evening meal, she always marked papers and planned lessons. Sometimes, she fell asleep in the light of the coal-oil lamp, with her head on the kitchen table.

Nellie put a feedbag on Bess, who was stamping her feet. Then she took out the hammock and settled in, fishing in her cloak pocket for Wes's letter. It was postmarked Sudbury. What on earth had happened to him? Had there been a train wreck? Now I'm starting to think like Mother, Nellie thought. Mother always predicted disaster — especially train disaster — when Nellie went out at night. Nellie laughed at herself. Of course, Wes was safe and sound. They would have heard by now if anything had happened. After all, the letter had been posted three weeks before. There must have been a delay somewhere.

CPR, heading east,
September 22, 1895.

Dear Nellie,

You may have a big laugh at me for writing so soon, but I have had only you in my thoughts ever since the train pulled out of Manitou. I switched trains in Winnipeg and got on this one. It will take me through to Toronto, though there'll be an hour's stopover in Sudbury while the train takes on supplies.

As the landscape has changed from prairie to muskeg to scrub to the majestic forests of northern Ontario, I have imagined you sitting next to me, continuing our conversation of yesterday. I just wish we'd had more time together this summer. But we were both so busy — you at the farm and I at the drugstore in Manitou. I should have tried harder to coax you away. I always seem to learn the hard way.

If my thoughts do not always follow each other logically, may I plead distraction? There is a young boy in front of me who keeps climbing up on the back of the seat. As soon as he catches sight of me, he sticks out his tongue and makes faces. You'd know how to handle him, but I feel it is best to say nothing. I hope his mother doesn't notice or there will be an explosion. The poor woman seems really worn out.

At any rate, I have been thinking about your views of God. You are quite right that I have taken on my father's ideas. He is a difficult man to contradict. You know what a firey Scotsman he is. You know how he believes in his mission as a minister. He has denounced governments and protested against the traffic in liquor. No one in our household has such strong views as he. Oh, yes, except for my mother with her convictions about the role of women. How I ended up in pharmacy is a mystery to me! Reaction to their very public life of ideas, I guess. I have views but I like to express them in private — more quietly.

Speaking of which, have you read John Ruskin on "womanhood"? He thinks women are made only to help, comfort, and inspire men. That's a noble cause, is it not? Surely there is not room for everyone to be active in the world. Someone has to keep the home fires burning while others go out and engage in public life.

This summer I heard lots of customers talk about these things. Not a few men came right out and said women should never be involved in public affairs because it makes them nervous. They said women should just work behind the scenes, where they can do the most good.

Nellie, you know that many people are afraid that communities will fall apart if women take on work outside the home. They don't seem to see that women can do just as much good or more by being involved in public affairs.

There is one problem, though, Nellie. And I want your response. If women are not suited to public life, should they be forced into that kind of work? Perhaps quieter women would prefer to stay at home. And many men like quiet women, don't they?

Well, the train's stopped at Sudbury now, so I'm going to hop out and mail this. I really would rather hear your answers to my questions in person. But that is not going to happen — until Christmas anyway. So letters it will be — as many as I can write. Look forward to your reply with great anticipation.

As ever,
Wes

Nellie folded the letter and put it back into its envelope. Then she took it out again and read the part about Wes wishing she was sitting next to him. She lay back in the hammock and imagined him doing just that — until she remembered the part about Ruskin and about some men preferring quiet women.

Nellie sat up with a jolt and began composing a reply in her head. How dare he make such remarks about women! Maybe he was just trying to get her goat. No matter, she would write him a response he would never forget. She fished in her pocket for the opal ring Wes had given her. She'd decided not to wear it on her finger after all. Too many questions would be asked. But she did want to keep it near her. Perhaps she would wear it around her neck so no one could see it.

Nellie felt a bit guilty resting in the hammock

and admiring her ring. At this moment Mother and Jack were slaving at their farm and kitchen chores. So many women would be working at this hour, as they did every hour of the day. And some, like Mrs. Sayers and Mrs. Wheeler from the old Hazel School district, had misery added to overwork. They were married to drunks, but neither of them had known about their husband's drinking before they married. A woman certainly had to be careful.

"Miss Mooney! Miss Mooney!"

What was that? Nellie thought as she repocketed the ring. It sounded like Jane Weber, but it couldn't be. All her pupils had gone home.

"Miss Mooney! Miss Mooney!"

It was Jane Weber. She was standing at the foot of the hammock, rolling her apron up around her hands and arms, and staring at Nellie. Her grey eyes were dark with worry.

Nellie sat up with a start. "Yes, Jane. What is it?"

"Do you think that you could come to see Ma?"

"Why do you want me to see your mother, Jane?"

"Because she's so tired all the time. There are too many of us and she's sick again. And she may get another baby soon. She always gets a baby before the last one can walk, and it makes her mad."

"I see."

"No, you don't see, Miss Mooney," or you wouldn't lie in the hammock every day after school. You see, Miss Mooney, she sees you here and it makes her worse mad. She says some people have all the luck. She never can get a rest because there are too many of us. Please, Miss Mooney, maybe you wouldn't go in the hammock no more . . . just for a while. My mother says hard things about you. It's because she's all tired out, Miss Mooney. Maybe it would make you mad, if you knew what she says."

"No, Jane, I would not be a bit mad," Nellie reassured the child. "And to prove it, I'll walk you back home now and see if I can help a little."

"Oh, Miss Mooney, that's wonderful!" Jane's eyes brightened.

As Nellie stood up, Jane took her hand. Together, they packed the hammock into the shed, stroked Bess's neck, and started across the school-yard towards the farm house just across the road.

Mrs. Weber was a bitter-tongued woman with a big family and a husband who was not really suited to the land. His family did not go hungry, but their clothes were patched and old. To make matters worse, Mrs. Weber refused to accept any help from her kindly neighbours.

When they reached the school gate, Jane said, "Please don't tell Ma I asked you." Then she ran ahead at lightning speed.

Nellie took her time closing and latching the school gate. Then she slowly walked down the road to the Webers' small, storey-and-a-half log cabin.

Going up the long lane to the house, Nellie wondered how Mrs. Weber had managed to see her in the hammock. The woman must have amazingly good eyesight, she thought, as she squinted back at the school. Then she turned and marched up the steps to the front door.

"Who can that be?" said a high-pitched voice

to the children inside. "Now get out that back door and shut up." Nellie could hear footsteps and thumping sounds. "And, Jane, take the baby with you." Jane was the oldest of the nine children. She probably spent a lot of time taking care of her sisters and brothers.

Nellie heard more steps, and a baby crying. Silence reigned for a few seconds before she heard Mrs. Weber shuffling towards the front door.

The door swung open. "Come in, Miss Mooney," Mrs. Weber said in her shrill voice. "I'm surprised to see you. Whatever brings you by here?"

Nellie stepped inside. There were no free chairs. They were all covered with children's clothing. Over the rusty stove hung a row of dirty diapers. They were drying, but no one seemed to have washed them. And there was no sign of any supper cooking.

Nellie's stomach churned from the smell as she said, "I visit all my pupils' homes from time to time. And since you're so close, I thought it was time I dropped in."

"Well, that's nice of you, Miss Mooney, but it's supper time and I haven't had a minute to prepare a thing. With nine children and another on the way, I never seem to get ahead."

"Maybe I could help."

"You? Help? How on earth could *you* help *me?*" She turned and picked up the drooling baby, who had crawled back inside the house. With a struggle, she propped the fat little boy onto her protruding stomach.

Nellie stared back at her in disbelief.

Mrs. Weber lifted her free left hand to wipe the straggling grey-brown hair back from her forehead and, frowning, she said, "I suppose Jane has set you up to this."

"I visit the parents of *all* my pupils."

"Yes, I suppose you do. And I suppose you hear a lot from time to time about all of us. Children have a way of talking."

Nellie said nothing. Instead, she reached out a hand for the sour-smelling baby, who turned away and clung even more tightly to his mother.

"Of course, I know I have too many children," Mrs. Weber said, patting the baby on its back. "And there are times when I get out of temper and wish I had never married. I've often said that if it were not for the clear disgrace of it, I would rather be a withered-up old maid like Miss Harris over at the Wawanesa School or . . . what you'll be some day, Miss Mooney. Now, thank you for offering to help. But my Bill wouldn't want me to accept charity — and especially from you. He's heard you have strange ideas. And besides, as I said before, what would you know about babies? Good day, Miss Mooney."

Nellie sighed and let herself out. Some women were their own worst enemies. Mrs. Weber was obviously exhausted, and yet she was too proud to accept help. Worse, though she envied Nellie, according to Jane, Mrs. Weber still felt superior to her — just because she was married.

It was going to be difficult to help women like that, Nellie thought as she headed back to the school.

6

"Well, I *am* glad you're going with Jack, Nellie."
Mrs. Mooney sighed as she stared at her daughter,
who was draped in sheets to look like a ghost.

"We're only going to a Young People's party,
Mother. And it's at the parsonage in Wawanesa.
What could be safer?"

"Well, it *is* Hallowe'en. And I must say, you look
ghastly in that old sheet. Now don't trip getting
into the buggy. I don't want you to sprain your
ankle again."

"Now, Mother, there's nothing to worry about,"
said Lizzie, who was standing beside Jack at the
door. She was holding Nellie's cloak and taking a
candied apple away from George, her four-year-
old. Lizzie had come to help Mother give out

candy to the few young ghosts and witches who would come calling.

"Here, George." Nellie gave her nephew a piece of maple sugar from the kitchen table. He had pulled the dish to the table's edge and was about to scatter everything on the floor.

"Now, Nellie, he just *had* a piece," said Mother. "He'll be sick if he eats too much." But George had already dived under the table and was gulping down his prize.

"It's all right, Mother. George eats so little candy, a few pieces won't hurt him."

"Lizzie, you always were soft. That's the way you're made. But mind you don't spoil him."

Nellie stifled a smart retort. Lizzie could hardly be accused of spoiling George. And if she did, there would be reason for it. Her first baby had died when he was only five days old. It was a miracle that she was able to have another child at all.

"Don't just stand there, Nellie," Jack grinned, taking his dark brown short-coat and cap from a peg at the door. "Get ready to depart. I'm heading to the stable to harness Barsac."

Lizzie smiled her sweet smile and draped Nellie's cloak over her shoulders.

"You look like a big green tree with petticoats, Aunt Nellie," said the boy under the table.

"I'm not a tree. I'm a ghost! You're supposed to be scared!"

"I'm not scared. I want some more candy!"

"Maybe the *ghost* should have some candy," Nellie said.

"Naaah! Ghosts don't eat candy."

Lizzie and Nellie grinned at each other, then smiled at George and Mother. To their surprise, Mother was smiling and her eyes were dancing. "I wish your father could see little George," she said in a rare sentimental moment.

The spell was broken in the next instant, however. Barsac was snorting at the kitchen door, which meant Jack was ready to leave. Nellie stepped out into the frosty air, holding up the hem of her ghost-suit. She put her foot onto the iron step of the buggy and hopped up beside Jack, her white sheet trailing over the side. "Let's hurry, Jack," she said. "I have to see Tom Simpson about our part of the program before it starts."

Jack smiled and gave the horse a slight tap with the reins. They sped over the hardened dirt road, for Barsac was a spirited trotter. Nellie knew Jack had brought his best horse and buggy because he planned to take Barbara home.

"Well, I don't want to be late, either," Jack said. "After all, I am the Y.P. president."

Half an hour later, Nellie and Jack drew up in front of the parsonage that was right beside the church. Nellie jumped out and hurried up the steps while Jack drove Barsac to the church shed.

Tom Simpson would be there already. The evening would not be the same if they didn't play the trick they'd planned. One day last week, Nellie had dropped into the drygoods store to work it out with him. Now she giggled, wondering what the response would be. She hadn't even told Jack about it.

She hurried up the front steps of the two-storey wooden house and raised her hand to knock. But the door opened briskly and the minister's wife said, "Come right in, Nellie."

"It's so kind of you to stay in for us tonight," Nellie said. The minister, who had three congregations under his care, always led a meeting in Glenboro on Thursday nights.

"Oh, I'm sure you girls could have managed the lunch, but I'll be needed upstairs to look after the babies." A few of the young couples were married, and had brought their children along.

"That's nice of you, Mrs. Prescott." Nellie hung her coat on the long hall rack.

The parlour was already quite filled. The young women were crowded together on the sofa, an ottoman, and an assortment of chairs. Several boys sat on the floor, leaving a few vacant seats. Nellie walked to the far side of the room and sat down on the space left at the end of the ottoman, right next to Barbara Wilkie, who was dressed up as Little Red Riding Hood.

In a few minutes, Jack came in and strode to the front to open the meeting. Jack was handsome, Nellie thought. No wonder the girls stopped talking whenever he started the meetings. All the same, Nellie despaired of his stiff appearance. Grey wool pants and a knitted brown short-coat did not make a very good Hallowe'en costume.

Still, Jack was probably the most eligible man there, and there were quite a few young women staring at him. But the only one he stared back at was Little Red Riding Hood.

Someone poked Nellie in the back. She turned around and recognized Wes's sister, whose name also happened to be Nellie, though the family called her Nell. She had come along with the Manitou group. She was dressed up as a cat, all black and with whiskers. But behind the whiskers was a warm smile that reminded Nellie of Wes.

Nellie moved back a row to sit beside Nell and visit a little. That way, she would not have to listen to Jack go through the minutes and the plans for Christmas. She could not stand his stuffed-shirt delivery. He was probably being so formal just to impress Little Red Riding Hood.

Nellie looked over at the Misses Wilkie. They were hanging on Jack's every boring word, and Barbara was even taking notes on a sheet of paper she'd set on top of her basket of goodies. There was a wolf's tail hanging from the back of the basket. Maybe Barbara will be good for Jack, Nellie thought. She does seem to have a sense of humour.

"Well, I'm glad that's over," Nellie whispered to Wes's sister as her brother finished his first comments.

"Nellie Mooney, I'm shocked at you. Your own brother."

"He's a wonderful brother . . . most of the time. But he's a deadly speaker."

"You didn't expect Disraeli for the reading of the minutes, did you? Meetings are boring. Ask my mother!"

"What are *you*, Nellie?" a voice came from behind her. "A covered wagon?"

"Tom Simpson, I will not stand such mockery,"

said Nellie, recognizing her partner-to-be-in-crime. "You're a fine one to talk. You look as if you've just escaped from the circus."

A tall, thin young man, Tom was wearing a flashy suit of dark purple, with a red cummerbund sash. On his head was a black silk top hat.

"I had to wear a costume like this if I was going to be a hyp —"

"Shhh," Nellie said, giving Tom a sharp sideways glance.

Most of the guests had gone to the kitchen. Roars of laughter came from that direction, as they bobbed for apples and even tried pinning the tail on the canvas donkey that Jack and Tom had tacked to the door.

Later, when the parsonage was buzzing with talk and a good many cakes and pies had been devoured, Jack announced, "Now, let's all find a place to sit and watch a little *hypnotism*." He smiled slyly. "It's Hallowe'en night, and Tom Simpson is going to try his hand at hypnotizing someone. Who'll be the first to volunteer?"

Nellie did not want to appear too eager. The others might realize it was all planned. So she waited a few moments, trying to look bored. She was sure no one was going to jump up very quickly.

"I'm new at this, but I'm very good at it," Tom said calmly as he stood up at the front now beside Jack. "I've been studying for months. There's nothing to fear." He adjusted his red sash and curved his finger at the side of his mouth as if he were twirling a moustache. Jack stepped over to the side, to give Tom the floor.

Just as Nellie had predicted, nearly everyone turned to look at their neighbours. Nellie's eyes darted around the room to catch the first sign of anyone starting to get up. If someone did, she would have to beat that person to the front. Otherwise, Tom's performance would be doomed.

"Well, if no one else wants to volunteer, I guess I will," Nellie finally drawled. She rose slowly from her seat, pulling off her ghost clothes and setting them down on the wooden arrow-backed chair with its engraved seat. She didn't want to trip at the most crucial moment. And anyway, she was wearing a pretty new red woollen dress that Mother had just made. It wouldn't hurt to give her friends the pleasure of seeing it!

Nellie could hear whispers as she walked to the front of the room. "She's always the brave one," said one person.

"More like the bold one," said another.

Well, she would show them, Nellie thought, as she walked between two rows of chairs, then passed more groups sitting on the dark-grey hooked mats at the side.

Reaching the front of the room, Nellie pretended to hesitate. In fact, she made a motion as if to go back to her seat.

"Don't be afraid, Nellie," Tom said. "Just turn around while I write out my plans on this slate. Of course, you can't see them."

Tom wrote on the slate, *Bring me a comb from the room upstairs where some of the ladies left their coats.* Then he held the words high and walked across the front of the room, carefully keeping the slate facing away from Nellie. "Does anyone want to come up closer to see the message?"

A few gasps and giggles came from the women. But no one came forward.

"That's okay, we'll trust the eyesight of the ladies on the sofa," said Stuart Humphreys from the back.

Then Tom erased the slate and handed it to a girl on the sofa for safekeeping.

Nellie's shoulders quivered a little as she stood in the far left corner of the parlour. She was starting to giggle. *Don't laugh now!* she said to herself, sucking in her cheeks to stop smiling.

"You may look around now," Tom commanded her. Nellie turned slowly, trying not to listen to the comments from the crowd.

"She's shaking!" one of the Wilkie girls said.

"Yeah, she's already in a trance," said Elick King from the hall stairs.

As Tom stared stonily at Nellie, her eyes gradually became more and more vacant. A strange silence fell upon the group of witches and fairy-tale characters as they watched. Elick had moved in from the hall to get a better view.

"Now, I shall give Nellie my message by thought waves," Tom announced. "But please remember, I'm new at this. I've been studying hypnotism for a long time, but I haven't actually tried it out on anyone before." Murmurs of protest rose from the young women on the sofa.

"It may not work at all, but I do need complete silence," Tom added with pretended humility.

The audience settled down immediately, for

they respected Tom's apparent honesty in admitting he was not a professional. They would help him out all they could.

Nellie had another great impulse to laugh, but she knew that if she did, she would ruin it all.

When she heard some movement in the audience, she decided it was time to perform. She walked slowly up the stairs to a room where some of the coats had been put and came down with a comb. Her expression never wavered.

The audience watched intently.

Jack had sat down beside Barbara now and shifted uneasily when Barbara gasped out loud, gazing at Nellie in awe.

Making the most of the situation, Tom said with some confidence, "Now, as you can see, Nellie is completely in my power. I can get her to do *anything* that I ask. Can't you tell by that vacant look? And that's what hypnotism is. It is the power of the stronger over the weaker. It can be used for evil, but it can also be used for good — to reform the weak." Tom's six-foot frame towered over Nellie's four feet eleven inches.

"Oh, Tom, I don't like the way she looks," Barbara gasped. Then she leaned over towards Jack and whispered, "Make him bring her out of it."

Making the most of *his* situation, Jack reached over and took Barbara's hand. "Don't worry, she'll be just fine."

Wes's sister, Nell, stared closely at Nellie and said, "Let's try one more!"

"I don't know," Tom said, trying to appear as if

he were in some doubt himself. "Maybe we shouldn't . . ."

"Oh, c'mon, Tom," Wes's sister said. After all, Nellie had boarded with them for three years when she was teaching in Manitou and Treherne. Nell knew some of Nellie's antics and hadn't been fooled by the shaking shoulders. She'd seen Nellie have a spasm of giggles before.

So Tom gently placed his hands on Nellie's shoulders and turned her around to face the front corner again. Then he wrote another command on his slate and waved it high in the air.

"Now I shall put Nellie into a deeper hypnotic sleep," he said in a slow, quiet voice. "She will not wake up until I allow it. Now . . ." He stared stonily at Nellie as he turned her around, sending his thought waves to her.

This time, the silence was interrupted with nervous throat clearing. Nellie's eyes had lost all focus, and a strange red flush burned over both her cheeks.

"I don't think this is a good idea," Barbara whispered to Jack. He squeezed her hand and still didn't seem concerned. Barbara watched Nellie's every move with worried eyes.

Nellie walked into the hall, reached up, took her coat from the rack, and put it on backwards — just as Tom had instructed.

"Okay, Tom," said Jack. "I think it's time you brought her back." He could see that Barbara and a few others were alarmed.

"Do you think you could make her sing?" asked Bob, who was sitting beside his wife, Violet, at the back of the dining room. He was not convinced she was really hypnotized. After all, she was the same girl who had once made him believe she'd seen a green wolf.

Tom rose to the bait but with some hesitation. "Well now, with more practice, I believe I could do that. But, you see, as I've told you all, I'm new at this sort of thing. Maybe by the next meeting I'll be able to do that."

Then Tom looked over at Jack and said, "I guess I should bring her around now. There are more items on the program. It's not fair to the others to take too long."

Jack smiled and nodded.

Tom stepped over to Nellie, whose vacant eyes were now wandering aimlessly around the room. Tom looked at Nellie closely, gravely. Then he clapped his hands right in front of her face.

Nellie was now having such a delightful time listening to all the comments that she decided to make the fun last a few more minutes.

She gazed straight ahead without blinking.

Tom swallowed and stared more closely at Nellie's vacant eyes. Was it possible that he really *had* hypnotized her? He stepped up to her and shook her. She went almost limp, but the vacant eyes never wavered.

"I didn't think you could do it. I thought she had a stronger mind than yours, Tom," Nell shouted out in panic. "Now, don't you know how to undo it?"

Tom was in too much panic himself to reply. He kept staring at Nellie, open-mouthed.

"Get a pail of water," Jack said, looking concerned. "That'll bring her 'round."

Really, Jack, Nellie thought, *I'll get you for that!*

Elick went to the kitchen, grabbed a bucket, and slipped out the side door. In a few minutes he returned and handed Jack a pail of freezing cold well water.

Jack raised the bucket above Nellie's head. "If she doesn't come out of it soon, we'll have to use the water treatment," he said, looking more delighted than concerned now. "Take her coat off, Tom," Jack ordered. Tom fumbled as he tried to take off the coat Nellie had put on backwards.

Nellie still stared ahead. She knew people would suspect fraud if she snapped out of the trance before the water was dumped on her.

"Time for the water treatment," Jack said, with brotherly glee. "This'll work. Don't you worry!"

He emptied the pail, and water ran down Nellie's head in rivulets. Her hair flattened into clumps along her neck, and her clothes clung to her limply. She was relieved Wes wasn't there!

"Oh, Jack," Barbara gasped.

Nell jumped up and started to mop the water off Nellie's face. "That was cruel, Jack, and it didn't do a bit of good. See! She's staring just as bad as ever. I'm scared!"

It was obvious now that Tom was in a panic. "I didn't know it would work like this," he said. He looked helpless as he slumped down into an empty seat in the front row.

Jack's eyebrows raised a little — Tom's concern was genuine, he could see that.

"Is there a doctor near here?" asked someone from Treesbank.

"Yes, that's it! Run for the doctor," said a young woman from Manitou.

"He's just two houses away," said Elick, who had brought the water so quickly. He jumped to his feet. "I'm on my way."

Nellie decided then that she'd better come out of the trance, in a hurry, for Dr. Lamont was one of the trustees for the local school board. She blinked slowly as though opening her eyes after a long sleep.

"Wait!" Jack said to Elick, who was already going out the back door. "She may be coming round."

Nellie stretched her arms and slowly let her eyes move from one anxious face in the audience to the next. Then, with pretended alarm, she clutched her wet head.

"Whatever happened?" she asked with horror. "My hair's all wet. And my clothes, too." She touched the front of her new red dress and squeezed some of the water out of the skirts.

"Are you all right?" Barbara whispered. She had become almost breathless with fright.

"Oh, I'm fine, I guess, but I sure would like to know who poured that water all over me."

"It was Jack," said a few voices from the audience.

"I believe it!" she said, giving her brother a nasty look.

Tom took out his handkerchief now and wiped his brow. "I'm cured. I'll never try that again," he said.

Jack gave Nellie a sharp look and sighed. He

did look more relaxed, though, as he stood up to announce the next number on the program.

Nellie sat down and started to shiver. She thought about asking the minister's wife for a change of clothing, but she didn't want her to know about what had happened in her parlour. Jack had had quite a time mopping up the water, and Nellie wanted to give the floor time to dry a bit more before the minister's wife saw it.

After Jack had introduced the next number — a duet by the Spring sisters from Manitou — he came over and nudged Nellie. "I'd best get you home now. You're shaking like a leaf."

"Oh, Jack, I'm all right."

"No, you're not. You know Mother's always worried about you going into pneumonia. And if you get so much as a bad cold, I'll never hear the end of it."

Jack steered Nellie out into the frosty night, after a long leavetaking with Barbara. Nellie shuddered in the cold air, but once she got under the old buffalo robe in the buggy she was almost steaming.

"You know, Nellie," Jack began, "sometime, you'll go too far."

"Whatever do you mean, Jack?" She was furious with Jack for pouring the water all over her. And now she had to go home before the evening's activities were done. She was not about to admit anything.

"You just don't know when to stop, do you?" Jack continued, "And you don't know your power over people. You were the one who had everybody in a spell. You were the hypnotist!"

"Even you looked worried!" Nellie said with a smug smile.

"Me! I'm surprised you could tell with your eyes so pulled out of focus. And what about Tom? He was in quite a state. Do you think you were fair to him?"

Suddenly Nellie felt a cold chill creeping through her in spite of the heavy buffalo robe. "Wow! I never even thought . . ." she said. "I just didn't think."

"Well, maybe it's time you did."

"I'll try," Nellie said. Now she was feeling completely miserable.

Jack gave Barsac's reins a little flip. "I'm going back to the meeting," he said, "and I'm not waiting for you to change your clothes."

Nellie knew he wanted to get back in time to drive Barbara home before someone else did. She looked out the side of the buggy so she wouldn't have to look at him.

"I was thinking of driving you to the Judd sisters' revival meetings later this month. But now I'm not so sure."

"Judd sisters?"

"Yes, a couple of female travelling evangelists."

"Oh, well, I don't really care."

Nellie took in deep breaths of the fresh, clear air. It was a beautiful night. And Lizzie was staying over. They would have a good long chat — after she wrote to Wes, that is. He had written her another letter after the one she'd read in the hammock, but she hadn't had time to reply.

****

When Nellie opened the back door, she was surprised to find that Lizzie and Mother had both gone to bed. Nap was snoring beside the stove and the clock was ticking. But otherwise, the house was silent. Nellie was relieved, for her hair was still wet. She took a big piece of red flannel from the cupboard drawer, then stood by the stove, rubbing her head. When her hair was almost dry, she tiptoed upstairs and slipped into her warm cotton nightgown. Then she came down again, sat at the kitchen table, and started her letter to Wes.

October 31, 1895.

Dear Wes,

You'll never guess what I did tonight. There was a Hallowe'en party at the Methodist parsonage in Wawanesa, and Tom and I played a trick. You must not tell anyone. You are sworn to secrecy. Tom claimed to have powers of hypnotism and proceeded to "hypnotize" me into doing things I had already planned with him. Everyone was quite deceived, I think — except my dear brother and Bob Ingram, of course.

Nellie decided it would be wise not to tell Wes about the pail of water. After all, there was no point in putting herself in a bad light.

Your sister was there, dressed as a cat. Very convincing. I was a ghost and so made a nice other half for Nell, she of the whiskers.

I hope you do know what great respect I have for your father. I may have differences of opinion with him, but I have nothing but admiration for his work. The church does not offer an easy life — but it appeals to the best in human nature. Like so many men of the cloth, your father is helping to shape society, to change lives for the better. Besides, I do not think your father's bright spirit is fully convinced by all that stern theology. Remember the time I left that "evil book," George du Maurier's Trilby on the hall table at the parsonage in Treherne? Remember how he succumbed to "temptation" and decided the book was not really so evil, after all? Underneath his tough theological hide, I believe your father is somewhat like mine. He always said that God was "good at forgetting" when we really are sorry for the sinful things we do.

Not that Christians are soft. By no means. The world is not a safe place, Wes. Just look at the women who marry men in good faith, then spend their lives with the drunken monsters. The job of Christians is to help people like that. And for such a task, they need to be tough, not soft.

And as for Ruskin, I must open my response with a resounding "Et tu, Brute!" You are a traitor, Wes McClung, you of the fine-sounding words, who claim to support me in my every quest. Yes, Ruskin agreed that women should be educated. But what for? Merely to be prepared to play a supporting role to their husbands and brothers. How would you feel if I wrote a book recommending that men be educated just to support the work and dreams of their wives and sisters?

I've read the preface to Ruskin's Sesame and Lilies and was quite sickened by his suggestion that girls "go into the families of the poor and . . . coax them into pretty and tidy ways, and plead for well-folded tablecloths." I wish Ruskin could have seen some of our farm women out here. They don't even have tablecloths, and if they *did, they wouldn't have time to fold them. Many of them work in the fields all day, then stay up half the night cooking and baking for the next morning. Meanwhile, their husbands sit by the fire or turn in by ten o'clock. Many farm women are beasts of burden in Manitoba.*

I go into the homes of the poor, Wes McClung, but not to teach women 'tidy ways.' What they need is education that will prepare them to speak up for themselves. What they need is the vote. That is the only way they will get enough political power to change their condition.

Also, I am deeply shocked by your suggestion that women should stay out of public life because it makes them nervous. I've seen a lot more men get nervous in the limelight. The reason powerful men do not want women to do certain kinds of public tasks is this: they do not want to share the glory!

And as for quiet women, well . . .

Nellie hesitated here. Was Wes dropping a large hint that he did not like Nellie's vocal ways? Was he really most interested in finding a quiet woman who would just darn his socks and serve him tea? Did he stay close to Nellie only because he found her a curiosity? Well, no matter, thought Nellie. I am who I am, and Wes will have to decide what he likes and dislikes about me.

As for quiet women, she pushed on, *no one is forcing them into politics. Just as no one forces a quiet man. The point is that the opportunity to work in the public sphere should be equally available to men and women.*

Besides, a vocal woman does not need to be unfeminine. Look no further than at your own mother. She is sweet, placid, serene. Her life flows on in endless song, above earth's lamentation. But she is no shrinking violet.

I could write so much more, Wes, but I must go off to bed. I'll write again soon, and in the meantime, tell me more about Toronto and how you find the life there.

Your friend forever (even if you have shown yourself to be a traitor),

Nellie L.

7

Nellie shut the front door of the school and smiled at Sarah. "Thank you for helping me put the lessons on the board. That saves a lot of work."

Sarah shivered in her shabby coat and the thin linen dress that was too small for her. The coat was obviously her mother's. The sleeves covered her hands, and its brown wool was threadbare around the wrists and shoulders.

"I love working for you, Miss Mooney, and Ma says I can stay and help anytime. I don't tell Pa, though." Sarah shoved her beet-red hands into the pockets of her coat. She had no mitts and no hat but would have to have them soon, for no one dared face the cold Manitoba weather without them. Even bare parts of faces had been known to freeze within minutes when the temperature reached forty below.

Nellie looked over to the shed where Bess was waiting to be hitched to the cutter. The fields beyond the shed were covered with snow, and a chilly mid-November wind rustled through the limbs of the Manitoba maple.

Nellie and Sarah walked into the school shed, where light shone through chinks in the log walls and onto the soft hay that lay on the floor. Nellie led Bess outside and hitched her to the cutter, then jumped up on the step and onto the seat. Sarah jumped up on the other side.

"Do you have many chores?" Nellie asked.

"Oh, the usual — gather the eggs, feed the chickens, and sometimes the pigs. Generally, too, I help Ma with the milking."

"How is she these days?"

"Fine, but she's very lonesome for Grandma, and now Grandpa's sick, she really wants to visit them."

"Do you think your father might be able to get the money for your trip?"

"No, he can't! Ma says it's no use at all — askin', I mean — 'cause there's just not enough. Miss Mooney, do you know what it's like when there's never enough?"

Nellie thought back and remembered very clearly what it was like. But it wasn't because either of her parents didn't try to provide for their children. In fact, Nellie's father and mother had deprived themselves of necessities for their children's sakes.

"When I want a new dress, there's never enough. When I want to buy another scribbler for drawing, there's never enough." Sarah was almost breathless, but her voice became louder and more vibrant. "But there's always enough when Pa wants to go to town. There's always enough to —" Sarah stared straight ahead, her slender chin jutting out.

"Stay in school, Sarah, and someday you *will* become a teacher. Just as you would like to. Then you'll have enough to take you and your Ma back to your grandparents — and you won't have to ask your Pa for anything."

"And I'll do that, Miss Mooney. Right now, I hope Ma lets me keep this dress you made me with the money I earned cleanin' boards for you."

Nellie's mother had objected at first when she learned that Nellie was sewing a dress for Sarah Sayers. "You'll never get that family out of trouble, Nellie," she'd said as she stirred a pot of stew on the stove. Nellie had spread out the royal blue wool and the emerald green collar fabric on the kitchen table. Her mouth was full of pins so she couldn't respond at first. But then she had explained to her mother that Sarah would maybe die of pneumonia if she did not have warm clothing for the winter.

"Well, then," Mother had said, "if you're helping a neighbour as a farm woman should, you're doing right. Just don't think you can change the world — or even that family, for all that."

Bess clipped along as Nellie stared out over the snow-covered fields between the school and the Sayers farm. No, Mother, she said to herself. I'm not going to change the Sayers by sewing a dress. But I might just change the world a bit if I try.

In fact, in two weeks, Nellie was going to start her career as a reformer. She had been asked to make a speech at a meeting of the Women's Christian Temperance Union. She had spent many happy hours in their debating room when she was teaching in Manitou. So a little speech would be easy. And she planned to make her talk exciting — not like Jack's introductions at the Young People's meetings.

Nellie looked sideways at Sarah. The girl had not seen the dress yet. She just knew it was in the package. Nellie could hardly wait to see her put it on.

Eleven-year-old Sarah was only in Senior Second. That meant she had four more years to go before she could try the exams for Normal School. She just *has* to be allowed to finish, Nellie thought — or she might never get away from her father's drinking.

Nellie hoped the dress would help Sarah feel more comfortable at school. Already she was starting to avoid other children, just the way her mother refused to visit with her neighbours. Nellie couldn't help wondering whether Mrs. Sayers had any more bruises to hide. Maybe that explained why she so often missed church on Sundays, though Sarah claimed it was because she caught a lot of colds.

"It's the next turn, Miss Mooney." Sarah was leaning forward with both elbows on her knees and her face in her hands, so Nellie couldn't tell what she was thinking.

Nellie had not been back to the Sayers' farm since she had sprained her ankle in the cowstable. She hadn't had a chance to talk with Mrs. Sayers — even at church. Sometimes Mr. Sayers sat with his family and sometimes he waited outside. But they always rushed out together after the service was over, never stopping to talk with anyone.

Both parents were obviously too embarrassed to face Nellie, and she didn't look forward to seeing them either. But for Sarah's sake, she had to.

Nellie turned into the Sayers' lane, stopped the cutter, and hitched Bess to the fence that ran up towards the road.

"I'm home," Sarah called out as she opened the front door and stepped inside. "And my teacher . . ."

Mrs. Sayers was standing just inside the door and had apparently seen them enter the house. She was even thinner than she had been two months before. Her face was a ghostly white, but there were no cuts or bruises. That incident had been an isolated one, Nellie hoped.

Mrs. Sayers' brows were puckered in a worried frown. "Is there a problem, Miss Mooney?" Although she was speaking to Nellie, she was staring at her daughter. "Is Sarah misbehavin'?"

"Oh, no," Mrs. Sayers. "In fact, she's been a great help. Thank you for allowing her to stay a little late each day to help me with the blackboards."

Mrs. Sayers relaxed a little and smiled at Sarah as she said, "Yes, she's a good worker." Then she stared over at the soup boiling on the stove with such an alert expression that Nellie wondered if it was about to boil over.

"Mrs. Sayers," Nellie began, then she too stared at the soup. She could see that Mrs. Sayers was not going to rescue it, so she continued, "To pay Sarah for her work these past weeks, I have made her a new dress." Actually, her mother had ended up doing most of the work on the dress — to Nellie's shame. However, she thought it best not to tell Mrs. Sayers that, so it would not look like charity — since Mother was known for helping the poor in their farm community.

Finally, Mrs. Sayers stared back at Nellie. "You've *what?*" she asked in surprise.

"I've made her a dress." Nellie drew the dress out of her bag. The royal blue and emerald green wool glowed in the rays of the afternoon sun beaming through the window.

"May I try it on, Ma?" Sarah asked eagerly.

"No, you may not!" Mrs. Sayers said, turning to Nellie. "Really, Miss Mooney, I know the worth of that dress! And the work my daughter has done these few weeks cannot possibly have covered it. Now I have a pot of soup to tend to."

"It adds up," Nellie replied ignoring Mrs. Sayers' dismissal. "And anyway, I really would like her to have this dress."

"I'm sorry, Miss Mooney. It was very kind of you. But we can't accept charity." She turned her back stiffly and stirred the soup.

Sarah stood next to the stove with great tears filling her eyes. Then, blinking them back, she held her head high and stuck out her chin as her voice broke the silence. "Then I'm not going back to school, Ma."

"Well then, you'll be able to help more around here," said Sarah's father, who had just walked in. He put his cap and coat on a nail by the door and sat down at the table. Obviously, he was ready for an early supper before chore time.

"Good day, Miss Mooney," he said in a congenial tone of voice, smiling at Nellie.

"Hello, Mr. Sayers," Nellie said. Was it possible he did not remember the barn incident? He didn't seem the least bit embarrassed or apologetic. Nellie decided to count on that. As Mrs. Sayers bustled around the stove, she turned to Mr. Sayers. "It's a busy time of year," she said.

"That it is, but we're ready," Mr. Sayers said. "We've plenty of vegetables and fruits stored. The potato, turnip, and carrot crops were all good this year — not to mention a bountiful wheat yield. No, sir, we'll not go hungry this year. The cellar's full." He seemed pleased with himself and in a very good mood. "Would you stay for supper, Miss Mooney?"

Nellie did not want to stay for supper, but she was reluctant to leave with Sarah's dress. Perhaps Mrs. Sayers would relent. "Well, I wouldn't want to put Mrs. Sayers to any extra bother."

Mr. Sayers smiled, "It's no bother. Get an extra bowl and plate for the table, Sarah. Have a seat, Miss Mooney. Now, tell me, how's Jack doing these days? It must be hard not having your father to advise him."

Nellie smiled, "Yes, it is hard, but Jack's a good farmer, and my brother Will lives with his family on the next half-section. He helps a lot."

"Yes, I hear you had a pretty fair yield. And Jack did well with his driving horses in the fall fairs."

"Yes, they won ribbons at Wawanesa and Manitou. Jack's proud of them, but the farm work keeps him too busy to spend as much time on them as he'd like."

"That's always the way with a farm. It seems a man can never catch up."

"Well, you might just as well stay for supper," said Mrs. Sayers, setting the pot of soup on the table. The aroma of carrots and beef filled the steamy kitchen air.

"Come to the table now, Sarah. Your teacher's staying for supper," Mr. Sayers said, looking kindly at his daughter.

Sarah sat down across from Nellie, her expression sad but somewhat hopeful.

Sayers and Nellie spoke of harvests and weather as they ate their soup. Not a word was said about the royal blue dress.

Dessert then appeared, in the form of preserves and thick slices of velvety homemade bread covered with tangy butter. The raspberries tasted nearly fresh. "How do you make these berries taste so good?" Nellie blurted out.

Mrs. Sayers laughed, then smiled at Nellie. "You mean you've lived on a farm all your life and you don't know this trick? The sooner fruit is prepared after it's picked, the better it tastes."

"I'll remember that," Nellie said. "That is, if I ever have a home of my own."

"Oh, you will, Miss Mooney. Never doubt that. You're a good-lookin' young lady."

Nellie thought with some shock that Mrs. Sayers sounded a bit condescending. Or were Mrs. Weber's comments still ringing in her ears?

When everyone finally stood up from the table, Nellie picked up a couple of plates and carried them to the side cupboard. She noticed the china was quite good — in fact, better than any in the Mooney household. Mrs. Sayers' parents had probably given her the set. Mr. Sayers could not likely afford such luxury.

"Now, don't worry yourself about the dishes, Miss Mooney. Sarah and I can handle them. I know you have work to do." Mrs. Sayers bustled over to the side cupboard with another load of plates.

Nellie was wondering how she could bring up the topic of the dress again. Should she do it in front of Mr. Sayers? Maybe not? And yet he seemed to be in a good mood. Still, she didn't want to cross Mrs. Sayers in the matter.

To Nellie's surprise, Sarah solved the problem for her. "Why can't I keep the dress, Ma?" she burst out. "I've earned it!"

"What's this about a dress?" Mr. Sayers asked. He was staring at his wife and daughter, who had both fallen silent.

"Sarah has been helping me at school, with chores after four — like filling the woodbox and cleaning boards," said Nellie. "Sometimes she even puts lessons on the board for the younger classes. Anyway, her time has built up, so instead of paying her cash, I made her a new dress. I really should have paid her the money. I can see that now." Nellie looked over at Mrs. Sayers in an apologetic manner. "But I needed the practice in sewing and I thought Sarah and her mother might like the dress." She paused. "May Sarah try it on and show you both?"

"By all means. Sarah, go and put it on." Mr. Sayers smiled at his daughter. Sarah grabbed the package from the chair where she had dropped it after her disagreement with her mother.

Mrs. Sayers lit a coal-oil lamp and set it on the table while Nellie sat and stared out the window. The sun had gone down and a few wisps of snow went floating by. Bess was snorting and swishing her tail restlessly. Nellie knew she should hurry home.

"Isn't it beautiful?" Sarah said, emerging from the bedroom. She twirled about on the hooked red mat in front of the stove. The light from the coal-oil lamp danced on the folds of the dress. Sarah's blonde hair bounced, and her deep blue eyes sparkled with energy. She will be beautiful some day, Nellie thought, as she stared at the girl, transformed by the power of a new dress.

"You do dress up well, young lady," said Mr. Sayers. "You'll be a credit to us yet. It's amazing how a new outfit can bring a sparkle into your eyes. Thank you, Miss Mooney, for the dress. It was right kindly of you." Mr. Sayers was beaming with fatherly pride.

Sarah ran and gave her father a hug, but she did not look at her mother. Nor did Nellie, who got up quickly and reached for her cloak on the nail by the door. She pulled it on, then turned to Mrs. Sayers.

"Thank you again for supper, Mrs. Sayers. It was nice of you to have me. Goodbye, Mr. Sayers. Goodbye, Sarah."

"We enjoyed having you, Nellie," Mrs. Sayers said quietly. There was no trace of resentment in her voice.

Nellie turned to open the door, but Sarah reached her first. She flung both arms around Nellie. "Thank you, thank you, Miss Mooney. I'll see you tomorrow in school."

Riding home, Nellie remembered again that it was not easy to help farm women. They were a proud lot — prouder even than their husbands — and would be beholden to no one. Still, when it came to watching their children suffer, shouldn't that be a different matter? Mrs. Sayers had even been willing to let her daughter quit school rather than accept the dress! But when her husband made the decision, she had given in. Like most farm women, thought Nellie, Mrs. Sayers was accustomed to being overruled by her husband.

What angered Nellie most, however, was the way these married women felt they were superior to single women. They would marry any man, even a drunk, just for the status. "Oh, you'll have a home, Miss Mooney . . . you're a good-lookin' young lady," Mrs. Sayers had said. Good-looking? Nellie snorted. What did that have to do with it? Beauty was in the eye of the beholder. Besides, she wanted a husband who would fall in love with her mind, not her looks.

And she wanted a husband who would not turn into a monster, the way Mr. Sayers often did.

Nellie's heart swelled with rage as she thought of the fine man Mr. Sayers had been that evening and the way he could be destroyed by his drinking.

The Wheelers were in the same situation. They'd sold their rundown farm, made a small profit, and moved to Wawanesa, where Mr. Wheeler had taken a job with the local blacksmith. For nine months, they'd been happy. Then Mr. Wheeler had started celebrating on New Year's Eve with a few friends, and he'd never stopped. He was back to his old drinking ways, and Mrs. Wheeler was supporting the family by taking in washing from the Wawanesa Hotel.

Nellie stared ahead into the darkness, more resolved than ever to continue her fight to ban alcohol. When she had lived in Manitou, she had joined the Women's Christian Temperance Union. They had a reading room above a general store, where women from Manitou and the surrounding area could come — sometimes just for an hour of quiet reading, away from their families. But at other times, they had rousing debates on the need for women to get the vote. Nellie had fared especially well one evening when she pointed to the vote as women's only hope for deliverance from drunken husbands. No women she knew ever drank, she argued. So with women in parliament, complete temperance would be possible. All taverns, including Charlie's Place, would be forced to close. Now, the Manitou group had rented a room above a restaurant in Wawanesa. They'd asked Nellie to build up a local WCTU. It was opening on the thirtieth of the month — two weeks from Saturday.

Nellie gazed into the gently falling snow, planning ways to hypnotize the WCTU. It should be easy, she thought. After all, hadn't she put the Young People under her spell on Hallowe'en? Even Tom had been convinced. Nellie still had not had the courage to confess that she'd tricked him.

"Whooaa! Watch where you're going!" Nellie was pulled abruptly out of her contemplations. A majestic roan loomed out of the darkness, pulling a cutter behind it. It was Mrs. Ingram again. Did that woman have some way of knowing when Nellie was visiting the Sayers? At least her husband, George, was with her this time. Then Nellie realized she must have come near the end of the Ingram's lane.

"Nellie L. Mooney, you are quite the lady. Out and about at all hours and no escort."

"Oh, Nancy," George interrupted, "Nellie's independent and perfectly capable of taking care of herself."

"Betty Jones wasn't, George. And our Nellie is like a daughter to us, you know."

Nellie raised her eyebrows in surprise. She now seemed to have been fully forgiven for her bad taste in not marrying the Ingrams' son.

"I'm just concerned for you," Mrs. Ingram went on, without waiting for a reply. George Ingram coughed but said nothing. "You know that little Betty Jones. Smart as a whip she was, but what trouble she's in now. A baby on the way and no father in sight. I suppose you haven't seen much of her at school lately, Nellie?"

Nellie looked at Mrs. Ingram without answering.

"Don't be so sure of yourself, young lady. It could happen to you, too, the way you gallivant around."

"Nancy!" George Ingram interrupted. "That'll be enough now. We have to get going."

"Oh, Nellie, I forgot to tell you. Dear Violet is having another baby. Right this minute. So we must rush on over there. I'm dying to know whether it's going to be a boy. Good to chat. Now, have a safe trip home."

Nellie pursed her lips and flipped the reins on Bess's back. So Betty Jones really was pregnant. She resolved to take her some schoolwork the very next day.

Then she rode off silently into the night.

8

13 Gerrard Street,
Toronto, Ontario.
Nov. 14, 1895.

Dear Nellie,

You saw right through my trickery! Of course, I do not approve of Ruskin's idea that women are made to inspire and support men. I was just trying to raise your ire. And I think I succeeded admirably.

Well, it's a busy life here, I can tell you. And I've met some interesting men and women. Jeff and Walter live here in this boarding house, and we often go out for coffee. The other day, Jeff and I met Mary and Pearl from the Normal School. They were such proper young ladies that they weren't going to speak to us at first, but then Walter came in, and it turns out he knows Pearl. She's from his home town. As you know, the Normal School

*trains the normalites to be very cautious and always
makes them dress up even to go downtown. If they were
seen without hat and gloves, they could face dismissal.
Well, after the formal introductions, we had a great time
talking at a mile a minute. They are delightful girls and
smart, too.*

He didn't need to sound quite so enthusiastic
about them, Nellie thought. Then she raised her
head and looked around. She was sitting in the
Wawanesa Methodist Church, re-reading an old
letter from Wes, and waiting for the Judd sisters'
Revival Meeting to begin.

Jack had driven her here, in spite of his threat
on Hallowe'en not to do so. But fortunately, he
was happily occupied with Barbara Wilkie. He was
calling on her a lot these days.

Nellie had already spoken to Bob, who was sitting with his father, and congratulated him on his
new son. Mrs. Ingram must still be helping Violet,
Nellie thought.

Barbara Wilkie was sitting with Jack a few rows
in front of Nellie to the left, and Tom Simpson
nodded from the other side of the room, but kept
his distance. None of Nellie's friends were as interesting as Wes's letter, so she had taken a back seat
to read and re-read it in peace.

*Toronto weather is certainly different than it is in the
West. Even though it's mid-November, I'm still wearing
my brown knitted coat. The trees are mostly bare, but
leaves are still blowing down the street. I can't believe
snow has not arrived yet.*

There's a different sound to the city. The horses clip-clop along the streets. They don't have the soft tread of horses on prairie roads. We have the luxury of a lake to the south, but I don't have much time to benefit from it. I seem to spend my time in the library, class, or back in my tiny attic room, studying. I have a nice view out my window, though, right down Gerrard Street.

I do miss the small communities back home, where everyone knows everyone else and folks always look out for each other.

Nellie wasn't sure if small communities *were* so good. She thought of poor Betty. Maybe in the city, she would not have had to hide in her home.

Now to respond to your thoughts on women being voted into Parliament. You know how much I support you, Nellie, in your desire for women to have the vote. If men and women are to receive justice as fellow citizens of the country, they must both have a say in how a country is run. People claim that wives influence the way their men vote. But who marks the secret ballot? Not the woman. So she can have little real influence on the man as he marks his X. Of course, the wife must therefore have the same opportunity to mark a ballot.

Does this mean, however, that women should have seats in Parliament? Some jobs are more suitable to men and others are more suitable to women. And I do not think that women would enjoy the fighting and the back-room dealings that are part of everyday life in government. Women can influence their representative, as long as they have power to vote him out of office if he does not cooperate.

You might be able to change my mind on this, Nellie. You have before. But I think that women need to attack one thing at a time. After all, Rome wasn't built in a day. The main objective right now is for women to get the vote. We can deal with Parliament later.

Nellie would demolish these flimsy arguments in her next letter. She would point out that if women had to rely on influencing male MPPs and MPs, it would be no better than influencing their husbands' votes in an election.

As for women being more suited to some jobs and men to others, she would cite the case of Mrs. Brown. She was a farmer's widow who had learned to do her husband's farmwork after he died. *And by the way," Nellie would add, "Mrs. Brown and I are organizing a new chapter of the WCTU at Wawanesa.*

Nellie looked up from Wes's letter, then folded it and stuffed it into her shiny black leather purse. She wondered whether Wes had really liked her last letter. She *had* been very straightforward with him.

Nellie's thoughts were interrupted by the sound of singing.

Softly and tenderly Jesus is calling,
Calling for you and for me,
See in the portals he's waiting and watching,
Watching for you and for me.

The meeting had already started and she hadn't even found the first song in the hymnbook. As she flipped through the book on the seat beside her, she caught a glimpse of two stunningly beautiful women at the front. They had to be the Judd sisters.

Nettie, the older sister, had a face like a cameo — delicate, sweet, and martyr-like — and eyes that burned with a blue flame. Maude was more of this earth, so most of the young men in the congregation had their eyes glued on her. Her hair was dark brown, curled back from her face, and her eyes were mistily purple, like dark lilacs. Maude was wearing a reddish-brown rough tweed, made with a little ripple around the basque and trimmed with a fringed ruching on the neck and sleeves. Nellie did not feel very much in the spirit, looking at them.

As Nellie was plotting a way to find a seamstress who could make a copy of Maude's outfit, the congregation suddenly stopped singing, and Nettie and Maude continued with a duet. Nettie's soprano voice, sweet and thin as a flute, ran up into the rafters of the church, and Maude's rolling contralto swept on like a cello.

Come home! Come home!
Ye that are weary come home.
Softly and tenderly Jesus is calling,
Calling, oh sinners, come home.

When Nettie stepped up to the pulpit, a silence fell over the crowd. Then she spoke in a gentle voice that carried to the far corners of the little room.

"We do well to be excited over the greatest

thing in life. Religion is greater than a horse race, or a football game, or an election . . . Excitement and emotions that have no outlet can be dangerous, I know, but religion gives an outlet. Christ said, 'Feed the hungry, clothe the naked, preach the gospel to the poor.' Have you any hungry, or naked, or poor, or erring, or discouraged, or lonely, or sad among you?"

As Nettie continued, Nellie felt both admiration and envy. She wished she could speak like that! But maybe she could. What techniques did Nettie use? She would figure them out and try them at the WCTU meeting. It was to be held next Saturday, December 7, now a mere eight days away.

Nellie was somewhat pleased that the church was full, in spite of the warnings of more conservative folks. Suspicious of the wild emotions that sometimes come out at revival meetings, they had warned people to stay away. But the independent farm people of Wawanesa did not take kindly to being told what to do, and the pews were crowded. A number of town folk had come, too. Some notable people had gone forward already during the meetings held on previous nights, and become believers. The evening before, the town druggist had given his testimony.

Just then Nellie noticed Mrs. Wheeler, the wife of the blacksmith shop worker who had started drinking again on New Year's Eve and never stopped. She was a very devout woman and had come to as many church meetings as she could manage, along with her nine children.

She walked straight up to the front and turned

to face the audience. Some people were still praying silently, but Nellie's eyes opened wider.

"I've come to ask for prayer for my husband,"
she said. "I hate to admit how much we need help,
but it is now past the point of my pride mattering.
John has refused to come to any of the meetings,
but I know that if you would pray for him, it could
make a difference. So I am pleading with you to
pray for my husband. Even a sinner like John can
be transformed by the power of God." As she
walked slowly to her seat, Nellie could see that
there wasn't a dry eye around her.

Well, Nellie decided, she did not intend to
waste any time in praying for that old reprobate.
He was hopeless. And as for his wife — such a tall,
pale husk of a woman, whose shabby clothes hung
on her like a scarecrow — Nellie felt a sort of pity
for her, but it was mixed with contempt. She was
such a doormat.

Nettie stood up to announce the last hymn, but
at that moment, the sound of heavy footsteps
could be heard at the back of the vestibule, and in
walked Mr. Wheeler. A strange hush fell over the
congregation. Was he drunk? Would he drag his
wife and children out of the meeting?

Mr. Wheeler marched right up to where his wife
was sitting with their nine children, and to the
relief of everyone, he sat down beside her.

Nettie looked out serenely over the audience,
and once again she quietly talked about God's
love and power, and repeated His desire for people to repent and turn to Him. Then she said,
"Let us sing one verse of the last hymn again."

The words floated softly over the congregation.

Come home! Come home!
Ye that are weary come home.
Softly and tenderly Jesus is calling,
Calling, oh sinners, come home.

"Now," Nettie said, "will you come?" She looked out over the heads of the people in the congregation, and everyone except Mr. Wheeler knew she was praying for him.

Suddenly, Mr. Wheeler rose from his seat, walked slowly to the front, and turned to face the audience. Only the crackling of the stovepipes above the box-stove broke the silence.

Then Mr. Wheeler began speaking. "I have been estranged from God," he said.

Doesn't need to tell us, Nellie thought. We know.

But Mr. Wheeler went on. "I have been a lazy good-for-nothing, letting my wife support me — and she has been a long-suffering angel."

Well, Nellie thought to herself, he's right there! She was starting to be interested.

Mr. Wheeler struck a handsome figure before the crowd and spoke with such eloquence that he had everyone's attention. "I accept Christ and I am through with liquor, so help me God." Then he marched straight back to his seat.

Nellie could see the skeptical looks on the faces of the people around her.

Then Nettie announced the final hymn, and the congregation rose to sing.

Amazing grace! How sweet the sound!
That saved a wretch like me!
I once was lost but now am found,
Was blind but now I see.

As she sang, Nellie began to feel a strange pity for Mrs. Wheeler that she had not experienced before. She doubted Mr. Wheeler's conversion, but she hoped she was wrong.

Then the meeting was over, and the room broke into busy chatting. Nellie could see that many had gone forward to shake Mr. Wheeler's hand. Mrs. Wheeler stood next to him, with tears streaming down her face.

As Nellie turned and headed for the door, she almost bumped into Jack and Barbara.

At the door, the Judd sisters stood beside the minister, shaking hands with everyone as they went out of the church. As Nellie whisked by, she couldn't help looking down at Nettie's feet. She was wearing the most exquisite pair of russet leather shoes. With a pang, Nellie thought of her own goatskin ones with the gap at the top. She smiled woodenly as she shook hands. Then she went on down the steps and hoped she would be able to hold the audience at the WCTU meeting even if she didn't have shoes like that. After all, what did shoes have to do with one's success as a speaker!

9

Nellie opened the door to the WCTU meeting room above the restaurant in Wawanesa. She'd bought new calfskin shoes, which now squeaked slightly as she made her way across the freshly varnished floor. Rows of wooden chairs borrowed from the Wawanesa Methodist Church were the only decor in the rather barren room.

It was quite a contrast to the upholstered atmosphere of the WCTU debating room in Manitou. As president-to-be of the Wawanesa chapter, Nellie made a note to raise money for comfortable furniture and bookshelves. She took out an important-looking black book and wrote a memo to herself, to that effect.

In addition to new shoes, Nellie had a whole new outfit for the occasion. She was rather proud of it. It was a straight-skirted suit of black wool with red facings, ordered from the Eaton's catalogue. She pressed the wool down over her hips as she made her way across the slippery new floor towards a group of early arrivals.

To Nellie's delight, one of those early birds was Mrs. McClung, Wes's mother. Now in her early fifties, Mrs. McClung was still beautiful. Her auburn hair, streaked with a few strands of grey, shone against her dark green velvet bonnet. She had removed her brown wool coat and made a striking figure in her elegant cashmere dress.

"Nellie!" Mrs. McClung took Nellie's hand in both of hers. "My dear, we've all missed you. When are you coming to visit?" She was smiling her sweet smile and gazing at Nellie with soft, adoring brown eyes.

"Perhaps when the holidays come. I've been so busy at school."

"Yes, you must be busy, with all the classes you teach. I don't know how you do it. But we miss you, dear. I hope you can come soon."

"We'd love to have you visit us at the farm," Nellie said.

"I *am* coming past Wawanesa with a friend in December. Maybe we might call then. My friend is visiting folks to the south of you."

"I'd love that, Mrs. McClung. We'll look for you — and your friend, too. Why don't you have dinner with us? Mother would be happy to have you."

Just then one of the ladies from Manitou hurried over and took Mrs. McClung's coat. "Mrs. McClung, would you please look at our agenda?"

Nellie was left to greet more women at the door.

Although many farmers and their wives came into Wawanesa to shop on a Saturday evening now that the harvest was in, it was still a little too early for some to have finished their chores. So Nellie was not disappointed that the room was empty though it was already 7:15. She was certain that more would come before 7:30, even if they were only curious. Speeches by upstart WCTU women were the only entertainment available on Saturday nights — apart from the drinking that went on at Charlie's Place.

As Nellie was moving towards the door, she ran into Mrs. Brown — and her five children, aged three to ten.

"How do you like the room, Nellie? Nice and clean, isn't it?" Mrs. Brown shouted as she settled her brood onto a row of chairs at the very back. Her face was tanned and weather-beaten, evidence of the long hours she had spent in the sun that summer. But she was neatly dressed, in a dark blue wool dress, and her grey hair was wound into a French knot at the nape of her neck.

"Now, Josh, you keep your sisters entertained," she said to the oldest boy. "I have to help Miss Mooney greet people at the door." Mrs. Brown stood beside Nellie and shook hands with the new arrivals.

Nellie was relieved because this gave her time to think about the speech she'd written. She hadn't been nervous all week, but for some reason she was a bit jittery now.

By 7:25, a dozen women were sitting together in

the middle of the room. There was still a feeling of great emptiness about the place. Some women doubtless stayed away because their husbands had forbidden them to come. And even Nellie's own mother refused to attend. She'd never liked the fact that Nellie had belonged to the Manitou temperance group, though she did approve of the temperance platform. "If they'd just stop there and not get into politics," Mother always said. Nellie hoped Lizzie would come, but she knew she couldn't count on it. Lizzie was always so busy with the farm work and with helping Mother.

Mrs. Ingram bustled in just before seven-thirty. "Land sakes, Nellie, you might have planned this meeting for 8:00. I don't think most women can make it any earlier — with all the chores we have to do."

"Maybe. But I'm not expecting many tonight anyway," Nellie said.

"Well, that's what *I* thought," Mrs. Ingram smiled knowingly, "but my George says that most husbands will send their wives along just to find out what you're up to. And I'd be careful, Nellie, you being the schoolteacher. It won't sit well with the trustees if you come up with too many radical ideas. So just let the others do the talking. That way you can't be quoted."

Nellie grimaced. "Really, Mrs. Ingram, I am quite in agreement with —"

"I'm just telling you this for your *own* good, Nellie," Mrs. Ingram interrupted. "Why, I've watched you since you were knee-high to a grasshopper — even before you could read.

Remember when I used to bring my Bob over to try to show you how to read? Your mother was so discouraged about you then!"

Mrs. Ingram *would* remind her of that just now. It did not make her feel any more confident. But she managed to say, civilly, "Please be seated, Mrs. Ingram."

"Well, I must say there's lots of choice for seats."

Mrs. Ingram took a good look at all the empty chairs and chose one near the back window, as far away from Mrs. Brown's children as she could. It was also a good place to see everything — inside as well as outside.

At 7:30, Mrs. McClung walked to the front of the room. Silence fell, only to be broken by the sound of clattering dishes from the restaurant below.

Mrs. McClung opened the meeting with graceful composure, as usual. Nellie wished she could speak as smoothly.

After the singing of the national anthem and the recitation of the WCTU pledges, Mrs. McClung looked at the small gathering and then up at the clock ticking on the wall at the side of the room. More soft footsteps could be heard coming up the stairs.

"Since folks are still coming," Mrs. McClung began, "I suggest that we have a good time singing. Would someone like to give me your favourite?"

To Nellie's surprise, Mrs. Weber spoke out. "'Onward Christian Soldiers,'" she suggested.

That suits her, Nellie thought as they launched into "Onward Christian soldiers, marching as to war." She's always at war with someone. Still, Nellie did like the song, too. Maybe, she thought, that's how the woman survives. She has to get into a fighting mood. Suddenly Nellie felt a tug of sympathy for Mrs. Weber.

To Nellie's relief, the next arrival was Lizzie. George was not with her, so Tom must be taking care of him. Unlike many farmer-husbands, Tom was very good to Lizzie and let her have time out by herself. Most of the women at the meeting had brought their young children with them. And to the credit of the women, the children were sitting quietly on their chairs — more quietly than they did in class, Nellie thought with some chagrin.

"Now, ladies," Mrs. McClung said, "we, the women of Manitou, are happy that you could come tonight, and we hope that you will come back. Although we are called the Women's Christian Temperance Union and our primary purpose is to promote abstinence and to fight the liquor laws, we do much more. We offer help to each other — whether it is just to provide a place to relax, or a bit of reading material for the soul. We are a group who support each other at all times. Now, are there any questions before we proceed with our meeting?"

Mrs. Ingram's hand shot up.

"Yes?" Mrs. McClung nodded to her.

"In my opinion, the church is the community support group that fills the need you just mentioned. You ought to know that, Mrs. McClung, being a minister's wife. So why do we need another group to do this work?"

"Not all women go to church," Mrs. McClung replied.

"Well, not many miss goin', an' if they do, maybe they deserve what's comin' to them," Mrs. Ingram retorted. She folded her arms and stared straight ahead.

Mrs. McClung flushed a little. "I'm sad to say that the church does not always meet the needs of women. In fact, women have very little to do with the running of the church. The boards are all made up of men — mostly fine men, but they take care of *their* concerns first. Of course," she continued, looking straight at Mrs. Ingram's averted eyes, "the men never mind letting the women take over raising money to build or extend church property. This past year in Wawanesa, the women's committees worked very hard to raise money for the new extension to the Methodist church building. They organized a fowl supper *every* month. The men kindly stepped back and let them run the whole show themselves."

A few heads were raised, and furtive smiles appeared on many faces. Even Mrs. Ingram's stern mouth twitched a little at the corners.

"Now, if there are no further questions, I would like to call on our first speaker." Mrs. McClung hesitated. No hands were raised, so she continued. "Mrs. Brown is a lady whom I admire greatly. Two years ago, her husband was killed suddenly in a tragic accident, but she has managed to keep her farm running very successfully. It has not been easy for her, with five small children. I would like you to hear about some of the trials that she has faced as a woman — alone."

Mrs. Brown laid her sleeping three-year-old daughter down across two chairs, while her ten-year-old, Josh, covered the child with his coat. Then Mrs. Brown walked slowly to the front and looked out over the audience. Her stern features relaxed a little as she smiled a welcome to the women in front of her — mostly farm women like herself.

"I knew nothing of business until my husband died," she said calmly. "I was a typical girl, trained well by my mother for life, or so I thought. When I married, I had already learned to bake and sew, make quilts, seed the garden, and milk the cows. But that was not enough when I became the head of the house with five mouths to feed. I had to do a man's work, as well as a woman's, and in doing that, I was surprised to find out things that I had never guessed before.

"Men are afraid of women, jealous of them, and unfair to them. They want women to be looking glasses for them — though false ones, to make them look bigger than they are."

A few women gasped and squirmed in their seats, but Mrs. Brown went on.

"Especially strong in most men is their dislike of women who know more than they do. I taught a hired man a new wrinkle about ploughing and he left me. He said he wasn't going to be bossed by a woman, and the neighbours thought he did exactly right. They would do a lot for me if I were a helpless, pretty little thing who burst into tears all the time, but they don't really want a woman to show strength. I cried plenty the first year I was left alone, and everyone was very kind to me then.

"But now that I am really trying to run my farm and look after my family without their help, I meet plenty of opposition. After all, everyone is very busy with their own farms. I don't like to impose, and anyway I can't keep on crying, even to get help. How I hate that song 'Men Must Work and Women Must Weep.'"

More gasps from the audience.

"I can work like a man. I can plough and run a binder. And believe me, my girls will get a man's education. You, too, might like to follow the business of running your farm more closely. Your girls might do very well with the training the school gives them if they want to be teachers or perhaps nurses, but if they wish to marry they will need more training in the business of the farm. Knowing how to cook, sew, and milk cows is not enough. If you prepare yourselves and your daughters, you won't be left helplessly floundering as I was."

Mrs. Brown ended her talk abruptly, stepped quietly to the back, and sat beside her children. Two of them were now sleeping soundly.

Mrs. McClung was again on her feet. "Our next speaker, Nellie Mooney, needs no introduction, for she is well known in this community. Our family first met her when she was teaching at the Hazel School, not far from Manitou, and then she came to board with us at the parsonage in Manitou and later in Treherne, when she was teaching there. We miss her this year, but our loss is your gain, for she is a fine teacher and was a great help both in the church and in our WCTU in Manitou."

Nellie was tingling with anticipation. She no longer felt nervous. She was going to give this audience news they had never heard before. They would be impressed with her dedication and knowledge. But she wasn't going to bore them the way Jack bored his listeners at Hallowe'en. She was going to sweep them away with images of freedom and a bright new future. She would go before them to throw open the doors of liberty, just as the Judd sisters had.

Nellie sprang from her seat and hurried to the front. Her shoes pinched a little, but she wasn't going to let that bother her. She did not carry a note, for she always detested speakers who read their messages. She was not going to read from a trembling paper. She would be funny, too. She would give these women a treat. A little humour was what was needed at the WCTU. Following Mrs. McClung's wonderful introduction, in a haze of anticipated glory, she faced her audience.

Nellie was surprised to see that the room was now crammed full of women and their children. The noise of washing dishes had died down below, for the restaurant was now closed. Silence filled the room.

Nellie opened her mouth to speak, but no words came out. The faces in front of her blurred, her throat went dry, and her tongue thickened. The silence thundered in her ears!

She could not speak. She could not remember any jokes at all. Why had this great silence fallen over her? Hadn't she given speeches before?

In the brief time that Nellie stood there, she

remembered delivering her speech about the evils of alcohol to the parents of Hazel School. But that had been different. Her students had presented their projects! She had only introduced them and later illustrated the doctors' charts purchased by the School Board. Now she had no students to back her up.

She dearly wished to see Tom Simpson walk into the room. Maybe he could hypnotize her. Or better yet, maybe there would be a small fire in the restaurant and everyone would have to leave the building. But no smoke billowed out from under the hall door.

Nellie swallowed hard. She felt an arm around her shoulders. "What is it, Nellie? Are you all right?" Mrs. McClung's kind voice came through the haze.

Gradually, the faces in the room came back into focus, and Nellie turned and nodded. At that moment, Mrs. McClung handed Nellie a glass of water that someone had brought to the front. She took a few mouthfuls and handed it back, feeling more like a doctor's patient than a crusader for women.

She could see the tired faces before her now, but she knew suddenly that the jokes she had prepared would do nothing to raise their spirits. She had forgotten her memorized words anyway, but she did remember why she was there. So she would tell them that simply. She would speak in her own words, whether prepared or not. Her speech might be hesitant, but at least she would say what was in her heart.

"We have to get the vote for women . . . on account of the laws. For only when women have the vote will prohibition become a reality. Educating folks about the evils of alcohol is not enough. I discovered *that* in my first school at Hazel, where I displayed and explained a doctors' chart the trustees had bought. At that Sunday afternoon meeting, everyone agreed about the evils of alcohol, but the next Saturday night, the same men got into the same drunken state as usual.

"I feel great sympathy and admiration for Mrs. Brown, who spoke so well here tonight, but it would be better, I believe, to have a good husband dead than have a bad husband living! The laws do nothing to protect women from their husbands, or from their husbands' taking everything from them after they have worked a lifetime for it. Here in Manitoba, it began with the Indian wives of white men. They were cut off from any claim on their husband's property. Now no woman in Manitoba has a claim on her husband's property. If a man wants to drink away his wife's livelihood, he is completely within the law. Nor does the church allow the wife to correct her husband on any account.

"Cleaning the dirt out of corners has always been women's work. If they had the vote, they could clean up the laws. Prohibition would be in place faster than you could say feather duster. And think what a thorough house cleaning would do for the Manitoba legislature!" A few women were smiling now.

"If women will back other women, they can and

will obtain the vote. Then — just think of the good that could be done in this fine, new country!"

As Nellie walked to her seat, silence fell over the room. Applause followed, but it did not last long.

Nellie smiled at the audience, but in her heart, she knew she'd been a complete failure. Yes, she was a teacher who talked every day in front of children. But obviously that was her limit. She would never be a real speaker — not even to women with half her education. Instead, she had just babbled away like the country girl she really was. So much for all her sophisticated dreams.

Nellie felt worse and worse as she thought of Jack and the Judd sisters. At least Jack had said something useful and logical. Nellie felt her new shoes pinching her toes as she remembered the Judd sisters with their perfect feet and voices, and their winning ways.

Now Mrs. McClung would never ask her to speak again. In fact, no one would ever ask her to speak again. And what if . . . what if Mrs. McClung told Wes what a clumsy speaker Nellie really was? Nellie shook her head to push away the thought.

The crushed president-to-be of the Wawanesa WCTU sat quietly through the rest of the meeting. She shook hands woodenly with the women as they went out the door. Mrs. Ingram gave her a strange look, but that made little difference. Nellie's misery was already complete.

As soon as she possibly could, Nellie gathered up her cloak and flew out the door to the stable where Bess was patiently standing. She was thankful she'd asked Jack not to wait for her. It would at least be a relief to feel the wind on her face as she rode home.

Why did you let me down, God? Nellie spoke into the comforting darkness. I was doing this partly for you, do you realize that? And you made sure my tongue got tied and my brain seized up like an old harvester. Bess snorted as if in agreement with her rider. God really should not have let this happen.

By the time Nellie reached Millford, she had decided to forget her high ideals. Better to buy lots of nice clothes, settle down, and marry. Better to forget this shining, thorny path winding up the hill. She looked up from the ground, which she'd been examining quite closely, to address God again. But as she was doing that, she noticed that she was coming up to the Jones' farm. Poor Betty, she thought. I have nothing to complain about. And in that instant, she decided to do one last good deed before she gave up her glorious mission.

A light was shining in the Jones' kitchen window, so Nellie knew the family had not yet gone to bed. She would stop and talk to Mrs. Jones. Perhaps the woman had changed her mind, and would allow Betty to do her lessons at home.

Nellie tied her horse to a low branch of a maple tree and walked briskly up to the side porch, where a tiny light was shining in the window. She knocked and waited.

The door opened and Mr. Jones thrust his head into the frozen air. "Just a minute," he mumbled when he saw who it was. "I'll call me wife." He left the door only slightly ajar, but Nellie could hear the hurried steps of someone leaving the room.

Then Mrs. Jones pulled the door open. "Come in, Nellie." With a tired smile, she motioned Nellie to a chair. "Won't you sit a spell while I get you a cup of tea?"

"Thank you," Nellie said. Mrs. Jones turned to the steaming kettle sitting at the front of the stove.

"It's nice to see you, Nellie," said Mr. Jones. "How's school coming along?" He seemed more secure with his wife getting the tea.

"Very well. In fact, I was just passing by and thought I should drop in to ask about Betty's lessons."

"Well, I, uh . . . wouldn't know 'bout that," he said. "The wife will talk to you 'bout that. If you'll please excuse me, I'm turnin' in. You know what it's like on the farm. I seem to be dog-tired these days." He got up and walked quietly from the room. Nellie couldn't help noticing how bent and old he appeared.

When Mrs. Jones came over to Nellie, she seemed much older than she had only a few months before. There was really no life in her eyes. "Mrs. Jones," Nellie said quietly after a few seconds, "if you're agreeable, I'd be happy to give Betty lessons at home."

Mrs. Jones poured water from the kettle into a bright white teapot on the stove. She opened her mouth to speak, then closed it again and sighed. "I'm sorry, Nellie," she said at last. "I do thank you for being concerned about Betty, but she won't be able to take lessons at home. She's not wanting anyone to see her."

Nellie nodded but said nothing.

"In fact," Mrs. Jones went on, "she could have stayed to see you, but she just ran out of the room. She hides whenever anyone comes near the farm. If it hadn't been dark, she would have hidden before you even knocked." Mrs. Jones sighed and poured Nellie a weak cup of tea. She set it down on the spotless red and white checkered table-cloth in front of Nellie. "I can understand how she feels, you know. I really don't want anyone to see her either."

The two women sat in silence for a while as Nellie sipped her tea. But when Nellie rose to go, Mrs. Jones gripped the young woman's hand in both of hers. "Thank you for calling, Nellie." There were tears in her eyes. Nellie wondered if anyone had called at this home since their trouble.

As she rode along the country road, Nellie raged as she thought about Betty. She remembered stopping at the Jones' farm the previous June. Betty, a happy, healthy girl then, was weeding a bed of marigolds. In her blue print dress and sunbonnet, and smiling, she looked as sweet as the summer day itself. Now she was a fugitive from society. And she would be forever. In this community, Betty and her child would carry the stigma of illegitimacy to their graves.

And what of the man who had seduced Betty? Everyone knew he was the father of the child. But he still went about town in style, driving his pacing horse and smoking his cigars. His lifestyle had changed not at all. Oh, yes, there would be a little whispering around him, but one day soon, that would pass. In a few years, he would probably marry, and all gossip about him would be forgotten.

The church authorities were no better than the gossiping townspeople. They had done nothing to console Betty and her elderly parents, treating them as outcasts instead. But no one, not even the church, confronted the man who was the father of Betty's child.

In her fury, Nellie dug her heels into Bess's side by mistake. The poor horse bolted, and Nellie went flying into a snowbank at the side of the road.

Uninjured by the fall, Nellie raised her head to see Bess clattering down the road, with her stirrups lashing her. Fortunately, Nellie was not far from home. She at least had a chance of arriving not long after Bess.

As Nellie walked along in the dark, she realized her sidesaddle had betrayed her. The things were uncomfortable for both rider and horse, but worse, they were unsafe. If she had been riding astride Bess, she would not have been thrown so easily. But astride in skirts! That was impossible. Even women's clothes were designed to limit them!

10

The Monday after her fiasco at the WCTU, Nellie opened the door to the Northfield School at half-past seven. The windows were starting to frost on the inside, and the blackboards had not been cleaned. The struggles of Friday had been carried over to Monday as if the weekend had never happened.

Nellie *wished* the weekend had never happened. How victorious she had felt on Friday as she swished out the door — like Joan of Arc, about to liberate her countrywomen from bondage. No time to clean the boards. No time to rake out the fire. Now she had returned, crushed by defeat, and she still had to clean up the school.

No matter, she said to herself. Fight today's battles today. First, she had to stoke the stove. Her brother Will usually started the school fire, but today he had gone to Winnipeg on business.

With the fire happily blazing, Nellie tried to concentrate on preparing for the day's lessons. But the disappointment of Saturday night still threatened to overwhelm her. She walked over to the stove for warmth, carrying a copy of *David Copperfield* which she was teaching to the Senior Fourth that day.

That made her even more depressed. Dickens was one of the authors who had inspired her to try to improve society. He had exposed the plight of the poor — orphans and factory workers in England at the beginning of the nineteenth century. Nellie had wanted to expose the plight of Canadian farm women at the *end* of the nineteenth century. But she was no Dickens. Saturday night had shown what a sham she really was.

God seemed to have pulled the mat out from under her. Unless . . . Perhaps He meant her to write! That was it! She would devote the rest of her life to writing novels about drunkenness and overwork on Canadian farms. Like Dickens, she would be a voice for the voiceless and a defender of the weak. She would write about people like Mrs. Brown and Sarah Sayers and Betty Jones, and make the whole world cry for them. Then, perhaps, justice would be done.

A great longing crept over Nellie as she bent her head and prayed that some day, in spite of her impulsiveness, she would be able to complete those plans.

Thump! Thump! Thump!

Nellie lifted her head and grasped the old railing around the stove. Who was knocking so loudly? And who would knock at all on a schoolhouse door? Students never knocked, nor did parents at this time of day. In a dazed state, she hurried to push open the heavy door.

There stood Mr. Best, the school inspector. He was a tall, thin man with a black moustache and deep-set, piercing eyes. Since he was new in the area this year, she had seen him only once before when he had delivered a lecture to students in Normal School. That had been over five years ago and she remembered nothing from his lecture.

Nellie stared up at him in shock. The rumour was that he had left the area and she'd assumed he'd forgotten to inspect her small country school.

"Good morning, Miss Mooney," he said politely, brushing past her with a huge bag in each hand.

Inwardly, Nellie groaned. The fire had started to smoke and was making a light fog around the room.

Mr. Best placed his bags on the low platform at the front of the classroom. Nellie reached for his coat, and flinging her own over a chair, hung his at the very front on the lone nail there. Then she stepped back and watched the inspector spread out some large posters and smaller papers on her desk.

He stood reading quietly while Nellie remembered that Friday's lessons, under Friday's date, were still on the blackboards. She shuffled a little uneasily at the thought and wondered how to approach the subject. She should be writing out today's lessons before her students came bursting through the door. But colourful posters now lay all over her desk and on top of the thick scribbler that held her lesson plans.

Mr. Best looked all around the room, ticking things off in his little black book. Finally, he peered at Nellie. "I was talking to one of your trustees recently," he said in a low tone, almost as though he were talking to himself.

"Oh?" said Nellie. "I wasn't aware of any problem."

"There's not any problem that I can see, but then that's why I come, isn't it? To make sure that there aren't any problems. As you know, Miss Mooney, each teacher must receive a rating, and this will be passed on to the local trustees and to the Ministry of Education in Winnipeg. We have all our teachers on record."

Nellie gave him a smile that she hoped was dignified but friendly.

"You have already been evaluated four times — each year in your previous schools. And I must say that your last two ratings were excellent."

Nellie already knew this, but she was glad *he* knew. She smiled widely now and said, "Thank you, Mr. Best. I do try my best — oops, I didn't mean to . . ."

"Oh, think nothing of it. Remember, I was a teacher for many years before I became an inspector. The children always play with their teachers' names. There are worse names for the game than Best. I bet you get called Miss Moon a lot. And that's a mild one, too. I've heard worse." He chuckled as he continued to stare about the room, making tick marks in his book.

When Mr. Best's eyes reached the blackboards, Nellie burst out, "I was just about to put today's lessons on the board." Friday's date was far too obvious for her to pretend the lessons were for Monday.

"I see," he said with a gallant wave of his hand towards the boards. "Well, don't let me detain you."

Nellie fumbled under Mr. Best's posters for her scribbler and, folding back the cover to the correct page, she stepped up onto the platform and approached the board.

Just then, Sarah burst into the room with Johnny Newell close behind her. Sarah ran up to Nellie but stopped short when she saw the tall man.

Looking at the large snowball imprints across the girl's coat, Nellie asked, "What is it, Sarah?"

The girl shook the snow from her hat and smiled. She looked almost robust this morning. "Good morning, Miss Mooney. Good morning, Sir. It's nothing really. Excuse me, I didn't mean to interrupt."

"You didn't, Sarah. Are you sure everything is all right?"

"Yes, quite sure. Thank you." Sarah turned and walked sedately over to the railing around the stove.

Nellie watched Johnny, who had now spotted the tall man at the front. He quietly took off his coat and mittens and threw them over the railing. Laughing, he said to Sarah as she came up beside him, "I've got the best spot, Sarah. And I've saved a place for your coat — right there beside mine."

Sarah smiled back shyly and threw her coat over the railing beside his.

Just as Nellie was ready to turn back to her blackboard, a fat hand reached out, grabbed Johnny's coat, and flung it to the floor. "You don't have the best spot anymore, Johnny," said the class bully, Henry Stead. Smiling at Sarah, he put his own coat beside hers.

Sarah glared up at Henry as she pulled her coat off the railing and held it folded in her arms.

"So you're too high and mighty to leave your coat by mine," Henry snarled. "I can't see what *you've* got to be proud about with a Pa who's the neighbourhood drunk!" He snatched her coat from her arms and threw it to the floor, where it landed on top of Johnny's.

Before Nellie could reach Henry, Johnny threw himself around the boy's legs. They collapsed onto the floor with Johnny on top of big Henry, who was trying frantically to kick him off.

By now Nellie had reached the scrappers. "Boys!" she said loudly. They looked up, startled to see their teacher standing right beside them. Johnny fell off Henry and both boys jumped to their feet.

"Henry, return Sarah's coat."

Henry stooped down to pick up the coat and tossed it lightly to Sarah. Her blue eyes looked even larger than usual in her thin, white face.

"Now, both of you, hang your coats on the rack."

Johnny snatched his off the floor and hung it up on the nearest nail along the back wall. Then he headed straight for his desk. Reluctantly,

Henry pulled his coat from the stove railing and carried it to the far side of the rack.

"Now take your seat this minute, Henry," Nellie said in a flustered tone. "And both of you boys start reading the next story in your reader." Henry gave Johnny a cold glare as he passed his desk on the way to his own.

Slowly Nellie walked past Johnny, and when she passed Henry, she leaned over and said, "You will remain after school today."

By this time, the school was full of students. Now that the fight was over, they had started their usual early morning chatter. Nellie felt she shouldn't take her eyes off them to turn around and write lessons on the board. She would just have to make do with what was there. Maybe she could review the lessons already taught.

Before the opening exercises, Nellie introduced Mr. Best as the area inspector from Winnipeg. Of course, every pupil in the school knew why he was there. Instantly, a silence fell over the students and the opening exercises were observed with great attentiveness.

"Miss Mooney," Mr. Best began, "I'd like to do the teaching today. I've rather missed it since I've been an inspector . . . and I do love to teach. I hope you don't mind. In fact, you go right ahead and put lessons on the board."

Nellie stared at the inspector in disbelief. Was he really going to teach? Hadn't he come to see her perform? Well, she guessed she had no choice. "Yes, certainly, Mr. Best," she replied. She picked up the lesson plans she had just put back on her desk and stepped up to the boards.

"Oh, Miss Mooney," Mr. Best said. Nellie turned around. What could he want now? "Be sure you put tomorrow's date on those lessons. I'll be teaching *all* day today."

Nellie rushed with the board work, for she wanted to watch everything. The lessons in her scribbler were all ready and she was speedy with a piece of chalk, so in no time at all, she was ready to watch Mr. Best work with her students.

She soon realized he was one of the most skilled teachers she had ever seen. From his bags, he drew out all kinds of interesting objects and pictures for every class. Hands were waving as if every pupil wanted to please him. Nellie could hardly believe the response. Only Henry looked on sulkily. But one time, even he forgot he was angry and answered a question.

Some of the least attentive pupils were sitting in spellbound silence when, at the end of the day, Mr. Best drew a reader from his bag and read them a story. There was no nudging, no shuffling, and not one student asked to go to the bathroom. Nellie was amazed and pleased, but couldn't help feeling a small twinge of jealousy. If only she could teach like that!

Finally, Mr. Best gave each class an assignment and motioned Nellie to the back of the room, where he invited her to sit down at the only empty seat. He balanced himself on a high stool, which Nellie sometimes used to sit on so she could see the whole room. Then he smiled. "Miss Mooney, I am most impressed. I shall be pleased to give you top rating. That'll be three 'excellents' in a row for you, won't it?"

Nellie stared at him in disbelief. "But, Mr. Best, how can you tell that I'm a good teacher? You didn't see me teach."

"I don't have to. Your pupils are the most advanced in my whole area, as well as the most eager. And they obviously enjoy school — very unusual in some rural communities. You have trained them well. There's my proof. I've seen some great lessons taught, but unless students are learning, they're useless."

"Thank you," Nellie murmured.

"And your discipline is excellent. I liked the way you handled the situation this morning — with prompt action."

Mr. Best packed his bags quickly, and then Nellie walked with him to the door in the outer vestibule. There he hesitated and said casually, "By the way, a trustee told me that you think women should have the vote."

Nellie gasped and held her breath for a second before she admitted, "Yes, I do, Mr. Best. I think they should."

"I agree," he said, solemnly. "And I hear you gave an excellent speech at the WCTU meeting in Wawanesa on Saturday." Nellie could hardly believe her ears. Who had told him it was excellent?

"I was speaking with Mrs. McClung on Sunday and she explained how well you did."

"Thank you, Mr. Best."

"I wish you luck in your work, Miss Mooney. You're doing very well." Then he lowered his voice to a whisper. "You may declare the rest of the day a holiday. Just give me time to get out of their way!"

He turned, then bounded down the steps, heading for the horse and cutter resting in the school shed.

Through the window, Nellie watched him hitch up his horse. Then she turned humbly and faced her class. "You have just made top marks — for your teacher," she said with a smile. "Thank you."

Unexpectedly, a cheer erupted from the students. Nellie gasped. Would Mr. Best think they were cheering his departure?

"Don't worry, Miss Mooney," said Johnny. "He's only a speck in the distance."

Well, he was more than a speck, Nellie thought, as she looked out the window, but he *was* beyond hearing.

Then Nellie looked at the clock. It was 2:00 p.m. "Now," she went on, "because you did so well with your lessons, Mr. Best has declared the rest of the day a holiday. You are dismissed."

This time, a roaring cheer followed and the class erupted into laughter and chatting. In a few minutes they had pushed and shoved each other out into the afternoon sun.

She never would be able to dismiss students in a dignified manner, Nellie decided. But then Mr. Best seemed to know that, for he'd asked to leave first. Maybe other teachers had the same problem.

Nellie was smiling to herself as she remembered Mr. Best's comment about women's votes. It was a good thing there were a few men like that. And Wes was one of them.

As Nellie wrapped a long scarf over her hat and around her collar, she suddenly remembered. She had asked Henry Stead to stay and he hadn't. Some disciplinarian she was! Now, how would she deal with him tomorrow?

The boy had obviously gone home to complain to his father, who was one of the trustees. It was the Stead farm that the Sayers rented and it was rumoured that Mr. Stead was not happy with the way Mr. Sayers was working the land. So Nellie would get no support from Stead for defending Sayers' daughter.

But she would stand her ground. Henry had no right to talk that way to Sarah. She certainly couldn't help what her father did. But Nellie knew most people wouldn't understand that. Children often suffered for their parents' shortcomings.

Now she'd also have to deal with Henry's father in the morning. Nellie stomped through the vestibule and out the door. When she turned to go to the shed for her horse, she saw Henry trudging *towards* the school. His brown hair was blowing out from under his cap and over his red face.

"I'm sorry, Miss Mooney," he said breathlessly. "I really did forget."

Nellie tried to look stern, but she felt elated. She wouldn't have a session in the morning with him and his father, after all. Maybe Henry wasn't such a bad child. She looked at him glumly, though, for she had been hoping to get home in time to go to Wawanesa with Jack to pick up the mail.

"Well, the important thing is that you came back. Now I want you to work on your next reading lesson," Nellie said as they walked back into the school.

Henry plunked down into his seat and took out his tattered reader. Nellie supposed it had been through many snowbanks. She did not imagine he used it much. He was a weak pupil.

After about fifteen minutes, Nellie grew impatient. The inspector had given them all a holiday, and *here she sat*. "You may read for me now, Henry," she said.

Henry looked up, surprised that she had asked him to read so soon. But he was eager to leave too, so he tried his best. His reading was no better than usual, but he finally managed to complete the assignment.

"You haven't been here very long, have you?" Nellie said.

"No, Miss."

"Do you think if I let you go now, your punishment will be enough to stop you behaving this way?"

"Oh, yes, Miss Mooney, I'm sure," Henry said eagerly.

Nellie barely kept from smiling. It was the first time he'd shown much enthusiasm in a long time. "Then you are dismissed," she said.

He wiggled out of his seat, grabbed his coat, and rushed to the door.

Nellie hurried outside, wondering if she should have kept him longer. Well, tomorrow she'd find out. Right now, she wanted to pick up her mail.

11

December 1, 1895.

Dear Nellie,

It's my turn to receive a letter from you, but I feel that I should write now, for I'll be busy nearer to exams. I have received nothing from you, Nellie, since the letter you wrote to me at the end of October.

Their letters had obviously crossed in the mail. It was frustrating sometimes, Nellie thought, the way mail took so long! You'd think there'd be a faster way to communicate. But then she'd best not think of sending a telegram, or all Wawanesa would hear about it by the end of the day.

I'm keeping that letter in my right-hand desk drawer and I pull it out from time to time. I've even read it to

*some of my friends. They rather like your arguments
about women in Parliament. Should I be opening my
own personal chapter of the WCTU here in T.O.? I seem
to be gaining converts to the cause . . . I should say our
cause, Nellie, since I believe in what you are doing.*

*You mentioned in your last letter that some men do not
like women who know more than they do. That may be
true of some men — but not of me. You know more than
I do about many issues, Nellie, but I like you all the
more for that. I don't know anyone like you, Nellie. I
don't think there is anyone else as clever and as devoted to
her fellowman as you — pardon me, I should have said
fellowwoman, but you know what I mean. I do admire
your great capacity to care for all people who need help.*

"Nellie!" Mother was shouting up the stairs.

"Yes, Mother?" Nellie shouted back down.

"Whatever is keeping you, Nellie? I need your
help *now*."

Nellie slipped the letter into the side of her
travelling valise where she kept her other letters
from Wes — as well as his opal ring. Then she
pushed the valise under the foot of her bed and
hurried down the steep stairs to the kitchen.
Nellie felt as if she was being scolded for being
late for school.

"Now, Nellie, hurry and put out our best china.
After all, a minister's wife must be dined in style
even if she doesn't seem to know a woman's place
in life. At least I know my duty."

Mrs. Mooney was putting her best china out on
the side cupboard. As Nellie had suggested, her
mother had written a letter to invite Mrs. McClung

to supper. This visit would be short, since Mrs. McClung was travelling with her friends Mr. and Mrs. LeRoy. They were on their way to see another friend south of the Mooney farm.

"That roast smells good enough for the queen," Jack said, sniffing loudly as he passed the stove. "But I suppose we'll all have to mind our manners when a minister's wife calls. I don't know if I'll be able to enjoy all this good cooking." He was gazing up at the fresh apple pies in the warming oven above the stove.

"Jack! As if you didn't enjoy good cooking all the time! And remember, I lived with the McClungs in the parsonage for four years, and their manners are much the same as ours. But the house is run differently." Nellie reached for her mother's dish rag to protect her hands and drew out the hot pork roast, then stabbed at it with a fork.

"Oh, yes, I think you've mentioned that before. How does it go again?" Jack sat down on the wooden stool by the door and began putting on his heavy work boots. "Oh, by the way, don't stab that poor roast to death. We have to eat it, you know."

Nellie pushed the roast back into the oven and turned to Jack. "Their three sons and daughter shared the household chores. Nell did not do all the dishes, all the beds, all the —"

"Well, pardon me, but how can I be making beds when I've got cows bawling to be milked?"

"Well, of course, you can't *now*, but in our younger years, when Will and Father did most of the outside work, you might have helped. You could have at least *learned how* to make a bed.

After all, I *learned how* to milk cows."

"Now, Nellie, stop arguing with your brother," Mrs. Mooney said with a sigh. "Set the table, then grab a paring knife and help me with these potatoes."

"And it's funny," Jack said, "that the McClungs' daughter has the same name as you. Didn't you find it confusing?"

"Not at all. They called her Nell and they called me Nellie or Nellie L."

"Yes, I remember Father starting that nickname for you. He used to call you Nellie L." Jack looked sadder than he had since he'd begun courting Barbara Wilkie.

"Because *my* name is Letitia," put in Mrs. Mooney.

"When my books are published, I shall insist that they print my name as Nellie L. Mooney, not just Nellie Mooney."

"Oh, yeah, sure," Jack said with a smile. "Good luck anyway, Nellie." He jumped up and grabbed the clean milk pails and pushed the back kitchen door open.

"Really, Nellie, I hope you'll never waste time writing novels! It's bad enough to be wasting your time *reading* them," Mrs. Mooney said. "Now, stop your daydreaming and help me. We've so much left to do before Mrs. McClung gets here."

Nellie started to set the kitchen table. She hoped Mrs. McClung wouldn't think it strange that they always ate in the kitchen. Her mother had spread out a fresh, white linen cloth with tatted lace trim around its edges, but it wasn't the same as eating in a dining room. They didn't even have a dining room.

"You put out one plate too many," Nellie said, as she carried the plates from the cupboard.

"No, I haven't. I've invited Nancy Ingram, too. George is going into a town meeting and she'll be alone. So I invited her over for supper. I told her about our other guest and she said she'd be happy to have a visit with the lady — but she's not signing any petition."

Nellie's heart sank. This was not going to be a visit. It was going to be an inquisition. She had been looking forward to a relaxing evening meal and a good chat alone with Mrs. McClung afterwards. Mrs. Ingram would spoil all that.

****

"Mrs. Mooney, I have never eaten such delicious apple pies. You must have a special recipe. I do hope you'll give it to me." Mrs. McClung smiled warmly at Nellie's mother.

"I never really use a recipe for apple pie," Letitia Mooney replied with her usual bluntness, "but I'll be happy to explain how I make them."

"Nellie, I do hope your mother has taught you to bake like this."

"Oh, she has," Nellie smiled impishly at her mother. "It's been a struggle — but finally I know how to bake most kinds of pies — cakes, too. I was slow at learning, but I quite like baking now."

"Nellie never used to be able to cook at all," said Mrs. Mooney. "But suddenly this fall, she took a real interest in learning. It's a marvel how Nellie will persist when she makes up her mind. But she didn't make these pies. She was at school all day, and I baked them fresh this afternoon. That's part of the secret, Mrs. McClung. My baking is always eaten when it's fresh. Jack sees to that."

"And I can understand why. You're lucky, young man, to have all this wonderful cooking."

"Yes, I know." Jack beamed at Mrs. McClung and held out his plate for another piece.

"Land sakes," Mrs. Ingram piped up from her side of the table. "Do you remember how stubborn Nellie used to be about learning new things? Remember how she couldn't read and my Bob came over to show her? But she just refused. Then they opened the new school and that teacher . . . What was his name, Nellie?"

"Mr. Schultz," Nellie said with a grim expression, for she knew what was coming next.

Jack took one look at Nellie, drew his red-checkered handkerchief from his pocket and blew his nose. He didn't have a cold. He was trying to stop himself from laughing out loud. Mrs. Ingram had told this same story many times.

"Anyway, Nellie couldn't read and she was a big girl. Was she ten or eleven, Lettie?"

"I believe she wasn't quite ten yet. She was ten when she started school."

"Well, anyway, that fall, it seems Mr. Schultz somehow persuaded her to try to learn to read. And would you believe it? The child was reading through the whole primer reader by Christmas."

Nellie rolled her eyes a little at Jack, who was looking down at his plate.

"Yes, she was a stubborn child," Mrs. Ingram continued. "Her mother thought she'd never learn to read. But where there's a will there's a way, eh, Nellie?"

"It's a bit the same with all of us, don't you think?" Mrs. McClung raised her eyebrows a little, giving Mrs. Ingram a studied gaze.

"Well, I, uh, wouldn't know about that. I am not an authority on folks' lives."

This time, Jack seemed to choke into his handkerchief. Nellie and Mrs. Mooney both stared at him — Nellie coldly and Mrs. Mooney indulgently.

Finally, he looked up and said, "Well, I hate to leave you ladies, but I still have chores to do. I hope you understand."

"Of course," Mrs. Mooney smiled at him. Jack could do no wrong in her eyes.

"Well, at least those of us from *farms* understand perfectly," said Mrs. Ingram.

Jack moved swiftly to the door, grabbed his coat and cap, and dashed outside without even putting them on.

Silence fell over the table for a few minutes. Then Mrs. Ingram cleared her throat and looked at Mrs. McClung. "Well, everyone around here knows I've always been one to speak my mind, Mrs. McClung, so I'll come right out with it. I have a few comments to make about your WCTU meeting in Wawanesa. I hope you don't mind."

"By all means, Mrs. Ingram, please tell me." Mrs. McClung set down her teacup carefully and looked up expectantly.

Nellie picked up her used teaspoon and started

tapping the table with it. Mrs. Mooney watched in silent pain as the tea stains began spreading out along the tablecloth.

Mrs. Ingram gave a sly smile and started in. "Quite frankly, I wasn't surprised by the meeting," she said. "I'd heard a lot about the WCTU, so I knew what to expect. But I must say, the discussion was off topic."

"Off topic?" Mrs. McClung looked slightly confused. "What do you mean by that?"

Before Mrs. Ingram could continue, Mrs. Mooney suggested that everyone move to the front room while she washed the dishes.

Mrs. McClung protested, and Mrs. Mooney was eventually persuaded to come to the front room, too. Mother was not the most comfortable in this room, but she had put a lot of work into it. The furniture was all festooned with Mother's best doilies, crocheted afghans, and hooked rugs.

Seated in a rocking chair covered with stuffed, red plaid cushions, Mrs. Ingram turned to Mrs. McClung and said, "Now back to the WCTU meeting."

"You were saying you were surprised by it." Mrs. McClung turned to Mrs. Ingram. "What were you suprised about?"

"I did not say I was surprised. I said I was *not* surprised." Mrs. Ingram was staring straight at Mrs. McClung now and tapping the arms of the rocking chair with her long fingers as she rocked. She seemed to be enjoying herself.

"Oh, I'm sorry," said Mrs. McClung. "Now, please tell me. What was it that you were *not sur-*

prised about?" Mrs. McClung leaned forward a little towards Mrs. Ingram and looked up at her attentively.

Nellie glanced over at her mother and saw her hands moving restlessly in her lap. Nellie knew she was uneasy.

"Well, they were talking about the place of women more than prohibition. It's as simple as that! They were off topic!"

"But the two are so closely connected. Women suffer the effects of alcohol. Even if we personally have not suffered from it, we all know some woman who has. And too often her children suffer, as well."

Nellie thought of Sarah Sayers and the Wheelers' children.

Mrs. Mooney cleared her throat to speak, and Nellie looked at her mother in surprise. "The Women's Christian Temperance Union started back in Ontario at Owen Sound, near where we first homesteaded." She turned to her daughter. "You were just a baby, then, Nellie. I always thought they were fighting a good cause — to obtain prohibition."

"And they still are, Mrs. Mooney," said Mrs. McClung. "That's our main purpose, and we try to educate the public about the evils of alcohol. But we have branched out since our early days."

"That's all well and good, Mrs. McClung," said Mrs. Ingram. "I never want to stand in the way of education."

"But we need more," said Mrs. McClung. "We need to change laws to bring about total prohibition in order to keep weaker individuals from temptation."

"Well, it'll be up to the men to change the laws. I don't see what we women can do about the law," Mrs. Mooney said.

"But we *can* do something! As a matter of fact, I carry my petition with me everywhere. Nellie, here, signed it long ago. If enough women demand the right to vote, we'll have the vote one day. Then we'll have some clout with our representatives in *Parliament.* We'll just say, 'Unless you stand for prohibition, you won't get my vote!' Now, if you two ladies would like to sign this petition — Nellie, bring me my purse, please. It's with my coat."

"Don't get it on my account," Mrs. Ingram said grandly.

"I won't sign either," said Mrs. Mooney, "for I don't approve of women trying to step out of their place."

"And where is a woman's place?" Mrs. McClung said in a low, quiet voice as she looked from one woman to the other.

"It's in the home — cooking, sewing . . ." said Mrs. Mooney.

"Not gallivanting around the country with petitions," Mrs. Ingram interrupted, "not crusading for women's rights while the husband and children are having to fend for themselves."

Nellie almost groaned again. Still she could see that Mrs. McClung was not disturbed. Nellie supposed that by now, she was used to such responses. It was Nellie's mother and Mrs. Ingram who were getting worked up over the conversation.

Mrs. McClung said in her usual gentle voice, "And what if a woman has no husband?"

"An extra woman in the house will always be a blessing," said Mrs. Mooney. "My cousin, Mrs. Smith from Ontario, is a widow and she came to keep house when I was sick and Nellie was away teaching in Treherne. We couldn't have managed without her. Now she's taking care of Will's wife's parents. Both have severe arthritis."

"And what will happen to her when *she's* old and has arthritis?"

"Oh, her daughter will take her in."

"And what if she had never married and didn't have a daughter?"

"Any one of her brothers would do their duty by her."

"That may be, but she would be depending on their charity — or that of her son-in-law. It's not a nice position to be in. As a minister's wife, I've seen some sad cases, where the family did *not* do their duty. And when they *do* behave as they should, all too often, they do it most begrudgingly. In fact, many women with large families, who helped to start and run businesses, still find themselves destitute in their old age. They are dependent on the very sons who inherited the business or farm they helped to build. Women should not have to rely on the charity of their menfolk. Married women should be able to own property."

"We seem to be off the topic of prohibition again," said Mrs. Ingram, "which was my complaint in the first place."

"Women should help other women in need

whether it is a matter of prohibition or not. That is just as important," Nellie said defiantly. Somehow, she hadn't been able to speak out until now, for it meant going against her mother. It had been an effort to break into the conversation.

If only Mrs. Ingram had not been invited. Nellie could feel her cheeks burning, for she knew her mother was staring at her with disapproval. But why should her mother have so much effect on her? After all, she had a perfect right to have her own opinion. She was no longer a child, and she had thought through her position many times.

Nellie knew that her mother still thought of her youngest as an easily swayed child — not as an experienced teacher, twenty-two years of age, quite old enough to have an educated opinion of her own on these matters. The days of her mother's telling her to hush her talk were over. But here she sat, feeling like a little girl again.

"Mrs. McClung is quite right," Nellie burst out, more loudly than she had intended, "in wanting to help women in more ways than in bringing in prohibition. If women had a right to the property they had earned, then they would not be dependent on the charity of their family. They would own their own land or businesses."

"And what would they do with it?" asked Mrs. Ingram. "I can't see you running a farm, Nellie."

"No, I suppose not," said Nellie. She lapsed into silence. Then she said, "But I would if I had to — just like our neighbour Mrs. Brown."

"Really, Nellie. You could never run a farm," Mrs. Mooney said. She gave Nellie a stony stare.

Nellie decided not to argue that point. But she knew she would give farming a good try if she had to — but only if she had to! It was the last thing she wanted to do.

Nellie was about to make a short speech on votes for women when she heard Jack stamping his boots in the kitchen. Then he appeared in the doorway of the front room. "Your ride's waiting, Mrs. McClung," he said.

"I am sorry, Mrs. Mooney . . . Mrs. Ingram. We were just beginning our discussion."

"Please stay for more tea — and ask the LeRoys to come in," Nellie begged.

"I'm afraid they'll be wanting to get back to Manitou. Mr. LeRoy has an appointment back in town first thing in the morning. So he didn't want to be late tonight. I was fortunate to have a few hours with you."

The women all followed Mrs. McClung into the kitchen. She threw on her brown wool coat, pushed a pearl hatpin into her felt hat, and hurried out the door.

Nellie stared from the kitchen window at the cutter going down the laneway. Like the fairy godmother in *Cinderella*, Mrs. McClung seemed to have come and gone before anyone noticed.

Nellie was furious. The visit had been ruined, thanks to Mother and Mrs. Ingram. Nellie realized that, secretly, she had been hoping Mrs. McClung would help bring Mother around to the cause. Ah, well, she consoled herself, she would just have to fight harder herself.

In the front room, Mrs. Ingram was still talking

to Mother. "I really can't see why she involves herself in all that stuff. You'd think she'd be busy enough, just being a good minister's wife. And I've heard rumblings, Lettie, from some of the Manitou congregation. They say her husband's a good, firey preacher, really knows the word, and speaks out with a strong message, but her — she's not too well liked. My cousin says. . ."

Nellie tiptoed past the front door on her way to the stairs. She had decided to go to her bedroom and finish reading Wes's letter. That would cheer her up.

The cold December sun shone through her bedroom window, making the glass sparkle like crystal. Nellie walked over to the dresser and took Wes's letter out of the valise.

I don't know anyone like you, Nellie. I don't think there is anyone else as clever and as devoted to her fellow-man as you . . .

Nellie smiled and read on:

Three of our professors have given us research assignments for the end of January. I can't possibly have them ready if I go home. I'm not even taking Christmas Day off. If I can't be at home, I might just as well be reading. So I'll sign out a pile of books from the library before it closes and bury myself in them for the holidays.

Nellie's smile turned to a frown. If Wes thought that highly of her, he would surely find a way to come home. He could read on the train just as easily as he could read at his boarding house. And if he came home, she would inspire him to work even harder. Nellie grimaced as she realized she was beginning to think like Ruskin, with his ideas of women acting as inspirations for men. She read on:

How dreadful to spend Christmas here! The boarding house will only give us leftovers, I'm sure, and the place will be empty as a tomb.

Good, Nellie thought ungenerously. If Wes lacks the sense to come home for Christmas, he deserves to feel miserable.

Well, I must say goodbye for now. Christmas exams start in another week. Like everyone else, I'm cramming. I wish I had you to listen to my Latin vocabulary. If you don't hear from me again before Christmas Day, please know that I'll be thinking of you and all the folks at home. Please give my regards to your family.

Warm regards,
Wes

"Warm regards!" Nellie threw the letter down on the dresser in disgust. Those were hardly the words of a man who thought she was the best and cleverest woman in the world. Surely by now Wes should have been signing his letters "Love."

Nellie walked over to the window to look out at the prairie. That was the best way she knew of getting out of a bad mood. As she gazed over the snowy fields towards the Brandon Hills, she realized, to her dismay, that she was truly in love with

Wes McClung. This had probably been the case for some time, but she had not wanted to admit it. Worse, he was probably not really in love with her. "Clever" and "devoted" were not words a man used to describe the woman he loved. Wes might just as well have been talking about his mother. Nothing to do with romance.

Nellie paced back to the dresser and re-read the first part of the letter. Then she read the last two lines. Bad writing style, she snorted, tossing the sheet back on the dresser. He's repeated the word "regards" twice in the space of two lines. Then, with remorse, she picked up the letter and put it back in the valise beside the opal ring.

There was nothing to do now but go out to the barn. Nellie tiptoed down the stairs, grabbed her cloak from the hook, and headed outside. As she dropped the latch on the barn door, she heard her mother calling out, "Nellie, where are you going? Jack's in the house now."

But Nellie didn't turn around. Inside the barn, she lit the lantern that always sat beside the door. She turned the wick down so it would not flare up and smoke the chimney. Then she hopped up to the platform between the cow stalls and plopped herself into a soft pile of hay. Jack spread the hay out there, just as Father had always done.

The cows chewed their cud on either side of her. What contentment! It was at least a consolation to be near them. But Nellie longed for Father. She wished she could tell him all about Mrs. McClung and about the WCTU and how things should be changed. He would have understood.

She could almost hear him saying, "But Nellie L., we can't upset your mother. She's a fine woman, a hard worker. A little bit stern like all the Scottish, but full of courage and backbone. Now, I'm different because I'm Irish. The Irish have had so much trouble, they've had to sing and dance and laugh and fight to keep their spirits up."

Shule, shule, shule, agra
It's time can only aise me woe . . .

Nellie started humming the tune Father used to sing. How did the rest go?

Since the lad o' me heart
From me did part . . .

Streams of tears ran down Nellie's face. She did not even try to wipe them away. Instead, she stood up and started dancing the Fisher's Hornpipe. That was the step Father had taught her out in the barn. "Strike into this one, Sparrowshins," he'd said. "Tap with your left and whirl on your right, and you'll have them all watching you!"

Nellie kicked up the straw as she twirled around, losing her troubles in the rhythm of the dance.

"Nellie? Are you all right?" It was Jack. What was he doing here? Nellie was mortified. Jack would never let her hear the end of it. Dancing in the barn in the middle of December.

"I'm fine," Nellie lied, repinning a lock of hair that had come loose.

"Aw, c'mon, Nell, you've been crying. I can tell. What's the matter?"

Nellie looked at Jack in disbelief. He really was unpredictable these days. One minute he was a big tease. The next minute, he was full of sympathy and understanding.

"All right, you've got me. I was crying because I miss Father."

Jack looked down at the floor in silence.

"He . . . he seems closest out here. I was just doing a dance he taught me. He was so . . ."

"I know. I miss him, too. Maybe even more than you do, Nell. He wasn't just my father, you know. He was my partner in business. I remember all the times he advised me about the farm. Most times we talked things over right out here, where you're sitting." Jack sat down on the hay next to his sister and picked up one of the kittens. Leonora, the barn cat Nellie called the Queen of Cats, had just had a new batch.

"Every time a cow is sick or I'm wondering whether to fallow or sow in a different field, I try to figure out what Father would have done. It's hard sometimes."

"You could ask Will."

"Yes, and I do sometimes, but Will has never taken to farming the way Father did. He's thinking of selling out. He wants me to buy his land."

"What!"

"Yes, he's thinking of moving into Winnipeg."

"Mother will hate to see him go."

"I will too, for we exchange chores and threshing. I'll be lost without him."

"If you did buy his land, would you be moving over to their house, Jack?" Nellie didn't like to think about it, for that would mean Jack wouldn't be around to help Mother.

"No, I don't think so," Jack said. "But —"

"Oh, good," Nellie interrupted.

"But I'm going to build a new brick house here on the other end of our property — nearer to the main road and Wawanesa."

"But, Jack, you know Mother will never agree to move. All her memories are here."

"Well, I'm not going to ask my bride to move into a house that is only an enlarged log cabin."

"Bride? Who said anything about a bride?"

"I'm going to marry Barbara, you know. We've been talking about it for a while now."

"Congratulations, Jack!" Nellie truly was happy that Jack had decided to marry Barbara. They obviously cared deeply for each other.

But Nellie had to admit she was not happy that Jack would be leaving. That meant she would be left alone with Mother.

"Well, I've got to comb down my horses," Jack said abruptly, back to his old self. "Cheer up, now. You have a bright future ahead of you."

"Thanks, Jack. I'm just fine."

Nellie watched him take the ladder down to the horse stable. Bright future? Yes, *Jack* had a bright future, but Nellie was not so sure of her own.

As she walked out of the barn and up the knoll to the house, she could see Mother standing at the kitchen window.

12

It was late February, and Nellie's view of the future had brightened considerably since that gloomy December afternoon in the barn. Jack and Barbara had announced that they would be married the following autumn when the new house was complete. In the spring, construction would begin. The old house was abustle with preparations. More important, Wes had written a long, dejected letter on Christmas Day, with quotations from Shakespeare and Browning and had signed it "Love." Since then, Nellie had written to him every week.

This snapping cold February afternoon, Nellie was re-reading Wes's most recent letter just after classes ended.

February 9, 1896.

Dear Nellie,

I'm sorry to be so far behind in my letter writing, but the load's been heavy! I'm glad you still write me every week.

March will bring more due dates for assignments, and also finals. So I'm afraid I can't promise to improve. But, just think, the exams will be over by early April and then, God willing, I'll be free and ready to practise my profession. I understand there's an opening coming up in Manitou for the drug store.

"Miss Mooney?"

Nellie stared up from Wes's letter at the thin face of Sarah Sayers, who was leaning against her desk. "Yes, what is it?" Nellie asked.

"Pa's taking us to the bonspiel tomorrow."

The child's eyes lit up a bit as Nellie smiled back. "Why, Sarah, that's wonderful." A number of curling teams would be competing at the bonspiel in Wawanesa.

Nellie knew that Sarah and her mother rarely went into town, and after her experience last fall, she couldn't help wondering how things were going at their home. Although Sarah seldom smiled, she did not have any bruises, and her schoolwork was progressing well.

But Nellie was not so sure about Sarah's mother, and she wished that Mr. Sayers could have been helped by the meetings the way Mr. Wheeler had. She felt a twinge of guilt over her skepticism at Mr. Wheeler's conversion.

To the surprise of most folks, Mr. Wheeler's new-found faith seemed to have stuck — at least so far. He had begun work the day after his conversion, in a lumberyard. He'd been received in the church the next Sunday morning on confession of faith. He became a new man with a new countenance, and was becoming one of the district's best-liked citizens. Still, only the years ahead would tell if it would last.

Nellie sighed, for she could hear Mrs. Ingram telling her mother, "That Sayers is a sad excuse for a human being. He's become a drinker in all seasons — not like the more civilized drinkers. And he'll even be drinking at harvest time this year. You mark my words! Everybody in the whole countryside knows about it. He'll come to no good end." Mrs. Ingram was a gossip, and growing worse.

Nellie stopped her thoughts and turned back to Sarah.

"We're going to have our pictures taken, too," the blonde-haired girl said eagerly, "while we're in town at the bonspiel." She was staring at Nellie, not certain her teacher had heard everything she said. "Grandpa's been very sick, and he's sent Ma the money to have our picture taken to send back to him. Grandma says he's afraid he'll not live to see Ma again."

"It'll be nice to have your picture taken, Sarah. Will that be before or after the bonspiel?"

"I don't know. Ma hopes he can take us as soon as we get into town, and I hope we don't have to wait." The worried look crept into Sarah's eyes.

"Maybe you could persuade your parents to go

to town early." Nellie knew that the bartender would be looking forward to a big crowd at his place after the games. And Mr. Sayers would be there before anyone else.

"Well, I've got the boards cleaned and the wood in, and I dusted off all the desks, Miss Mooney."

Nellie pushed Wes's letter into its envelope and then placed it inside her lesson scribbler. "I can give you a ride if you like. I'm leaving now, too. I'll come early on Monday to put my lessons on the board."

Sarah smiled again. Nellie thought it was a shame she smiled so seldom. She was very thin, but one day she would become a beautiful young woman if she had a chance to learn to take care of herself.

It was icy-cold outside, so once they were in the cutter, Nellie and Sarah pulled the buffalo robe up over their laps and around their legs. The snow crunched under the horse's feet, and the sleigh bells made a merry sound in the crisp air of this last Friday of February, 1896.

The horse sped over the well-packed road, and about five minutes later, Nellie drew the cutter to a halt in front of the Sayers' laneway. Sarah jumped down and stood waving as Nellie rode away.

Nellie sighed as she thought about Sarah's hopes for the following day. She was afraid for her. How inescapable are our family connections, she thought. We cannot choose what family we are born into, but we find ourselves there, bound for-ever, helped or hampered, by a relationship that was forced upon us.

****

Jack pulled the horses to a halt at the back door of the hotel. "Here, Nellie, hold the reins." He tipped and twirled a large milk can to move it more easily along the edge of the flat sleigh. He lifted it down to the ground, then twirled it right up to the closed door and knocked.

A hand appeared at the door. It grabbed one side of the can while Jack lifted the other. Then both men and the can of milk disappeared inside. In a minute, Jack was outside again. He took a few running steps and leapt up into the wagon, grabbing the reins from Nellie.

"Wait, Jack," Nellie yelled, jumping down from the sleigh. "I'm going in there. I'll be right back."

"Don't be daft, Nellie. What on earth would you —"

Nellie opened the door and entered a long hallway. She marched forward, wondering a little at her own boldness. As she reached the end of the hallway, she came into a lighted area. No doubt this was the bar, for she was standing at the back of a long counter. Rows of bottles were stashed underneath.

A man with dark brown hair and a bushy moustache turned and noticed her. "Miss Mooney," he said, his eyes widening, "your brother's just left."

"I know. I'm looking for the owner of this bar," Nellie said. She knew that the man before her was the owner, but she wanted to make him identify himself.

"I am the owner of the hotel and . . . the bar."

"Then I am going to ask a favour."

"A favour?" He smiled now in a friendly way. He donated money to a number of organizations in town. He liked his benevolent image. "What favour could I — Oh, I suppose it's uniforms for the school children. Well, Miss, I just could do that, but mind you, they would have to have my name embroidered on them."

Nellie could hardly contain her fury. His name, indeed! On children's shirts! Still she knew she must control herself if her request was to be granted.

"I am going to ask you to refuse liquor to one of your customers, just for this morning. Please don't serve him until this afternoon."

Mr. Bromley's large lips fell open and his bushy eyebrows lifted. Then he threw back his head and roared with laughter. "Well, I can't see myself refusing business. I'd get nowhere that way, Miss."

"I doubt you'll be missing out on any cash. For I don't believe he has any. But I suppose you give credit to some of your drinking customers."

"It all depends. I know the ones who'll pay and those who won't."

"Well, it's Mr. Sayers. He's the father of one of my pupils. Mrs. Sayers has arranged to have a family picture taken this morning to send home to her folks. Her father's ailing and may not last long. So she's sending the picture. Sarah says they are all going to try to smile, so her grandpa will know they're a happy family. You see, Sarah's never met him. They could never afford to go back even for a short visit because they never have any extra money, Mr. Bromley." Nellie stared him straight in the face and added, "I believe you have it all."

The smile dropped from the hotelkeeper's face. He stroked his chin as he looked down and then away from Nellie's piercing, pleading eyes.

"Hmmm, I'll see what I can do. But Sayers always pays his debts even if I have to wait some time. I hate to refuse a man like that."

"But couldn't you just make some excuse that you were low on whatever it is he wants?"

"The man's not particular. He'll take anything."

"Oh, I'm sure you could think of some clever way to delay him — at least until the afternoon. Couldn't you, Mr. Bromley, please? I've heard you're a very smart businessman." From her height of almost five feet, Nellie looked up at the towering fellow in the most pleading fashion.

Mr. Bromley wasn't sure that "smart", coming from Nellie, was really a compliment, but he did figure he was something of a ladies' man. So he gave her a wink and said, "I'll see what I can do for a fine young lady. Yes, I'll try my best. I always try to be a gentleman to the ladies."

"Thank you, Mr. Bromley," Nellie said. Then she turned and walked briskly to the outside door.

She was thankful it was so early and no one had been in the bar apart from John, the assistant, who was sweeping the floor. He was the same John who was the father of Betty's unborn child. She had a strong desire to rush back in there and tear his eyes out. No one had seen that poor girl for weeks now.

The horses were snorting a little as Nellie hopped up beside Jack. Without a word, he flipped the reins and they were off down the road.

"They're restless this morning," he said. "There may be a storm brewing."

"But the sky is clear."

"That can change suddenly."

"Don't be a pessimist, Jack. It's going to be a great day — cold, but look at the sun." She was glad he hadn't asked about her stop at the bar. He was probably afraid to find out what she was up to.

When they reached the rink, the games had already started. Jack drew the horses to a halt, and Nellie hopped down from the sleigh. "I'll see you later," he said. "I have to hurry back. I'm a substitute, you know."

Nellie headed towards the small cabin at the foot of the ice rink.

Inside the long, narrow waiting room, Nellie was surrounded by joyful sounds of laughter and chatting. Mrs. Ingram was talking to Mrs. Burnett as both women stretched their hands over the pot-bellied stove.

"Wawanesa will win!" Mrs. Ingram announced in a loud voice, faithful to the home team, as always. "We'll be going to Winnipeg for the provincial playoffs. I guarantee it." She was especially proud of the team because her son, Bob, was the skip.

"Well, if we do win," Mrs. Burnett was saying, "every man, woman and child will go to see our boys play in Winnipeg. But I'm not so sure we're going to make it, Nancy. Manitou and Treherne both have strong teams."

"Well, we'd better get out there and do our part. I suppose I won't have a voice left, come the end of the game. But my George says it will be worth it to have me cheer the boys on — no sacrifice too great, he says."

Nellie smiled as she wondered how difficult it would be for Mr. Ingram to withstand the silence, since he seldom experienced any. She sat on a side bench and looked at people as they filtered out to watch the games.

As the crowd thinned, Nellie caught sight of Sarah across the room. The young girl came flying over to her side. "We had our pictures taken and everything went fine!"

"That's wonderful, Sarah. Did you smile like that in the picture?"

"Oh, I did, Miss Mooney." A flush of joy spread across Sarah's cheeks. Nellie thought the girl looked like a rose ready to bloom.

"I must go now," Sarah said. "Ma's watching the games. But I came to tell you. I didn't see you outside, so I thought I'd find you in here."

"We can go out together," Nellie smiled.

They walked to the door and stepped out into the cold air. A raw wind had risen during the short time Nellie had been inside. She looked up at the sky and saw threatening clouds to the northwest. Maybe Jack had been right.

Sarah walked along beside her, and Nellie saw Mrs. Sayers standing by herself at the far end of the rink. "I guess I'd better go," Sarah said. "Ma's all alone. Pa's coming back soon, though. He's leaving the horses in the stable at the hotel. Says they'll be warmer there, and it's a short walk over."

Nellie felt a cold chill pass through her body. Would Mr. Bromley keep his promise not to sell

Mr. Sayers anything until the afternoon? Would the day be spoiled after all? Well, at least the picture had been taken.

The curling had already started. Wawanesa was slightly behind Treherne, and Manitou was leading against Holland. Nellie wished that Wes were there. He'd be cheering for Manitou and she'd be cheering for Wawanesa. But what would happen if Wawanesa came up against Manitou? It really wouldn't matter. It would all be good fun. Wes was a fair fighter, and she knew she'd sooner disagree with Wes than agree with anyone else. But did he really feel the same way? Would he be able to stand her fighting nature close up?

Though Nellie was writing to Wes every week, his letters were coming less frequently now — only about once a month. He still said he looked forward to her letters, but . . .

Was he really so busy? she wondered. After all, in spite of all her high dreams of doing great things, she was just a country girl. She had taken no university courses — unlike her sister Hannah. How could she hope to compete with the elegance of Toronto women? What chance had she against those rich and brilliant university girls?

"C'mon, Bob! You can make that shot!" Mrs. Ingram shouted at her son. Nellie's thoughts returned to the game.

Silence fell over the crowd, and every eye was rivetted on Bob. He took careful aim and delivered the stone, but his first and second failed to sweep it into the house far enough to count.

"Hello, Nellie." Barbara greeted Nellie cheerily,

coming up beside her. "How's the game going?"

"The game's tied and going into the last end," Nellie said.

Taking Barbara's hand, Jack squeezed in beside her and Nellie. Mrs. Ingram leaned over and grinned at Barbara. "Well, our boys are getting warmed up. We'll soon be ahead." She was not discouraged by her son's poor shot.

"Is that so, Mrs. Ingram?" Jack laughed. "I'll just bet you're right!"

A silence fell again as Treherne's skip settled down into the hack for his last shot. His third held the broom in place, and the skip came sliding out of the hack in delivering his rock.

They watched breathlessly as the stone came close, curled in, and settled beside their other one. The only two stones now in the house were very close to the centre button.

Bob, as skip of the team, would have the last shot, but he would need to hit both rocks out to win. This time, as he came to the hack, Mrs. Ingram drew in her breath and said not a word. She did not raise her eyes from her son.

Bob stood for a minute gazing down the ice. Finally, he took steady aim and threw his stone. Then a smile spread slowly across his face.

This stone needed no sweeping, for it seemed to be gathering speed as it collided with both Treherne rocks, sending them out of the house. Only the Wawanesa rock was left to count. A mighty cheer rose from the sidelines.

Mrs. Ingram's screeching voice rose above the rest: "Hurray for Bobbie!"

13

"Where would you ladies like to go for dinner?" Jack asked, as though he had all the money in the world.

The spectators were thinning out now, for the church ladies were serving home-cooked lunches in the parsonages of both churches. The hotel dining room was also open, so people were heading in that direction, too.

Jack was looking at Barbara, but Nellie smiled and said, "The hotel, of course. I hear they've planned double courses."

Jack sobered and gave her a cold stare. She knew he didn't want to spend that much money — at least not on a meal for his sister.

"I'd rather go to one of the parsonages," Barbara said generously. "I always think the ladies make much tastier meals."

Jack was all smiles now. "Yes, especially the homemade pies. The ladies make the best pies."

"Jack ought to know. He had five pieces at our last church social." Nellie's eyes twinkled as Jack scowled.

****

Returning to the rink after the meal, Nellie went to look for Sarah. But the girl was nowhere to be found — not even in the waiting room by the rink.

Mrs. Ingram had been right about the teams from Wawanesa. They were still in the competition.

As Nellie gave up her search, a cheer went up again. She'd just missed the completion of an end. The Wawanesa team was playing against Holland now, and the local crowd was a happy one. There would be a lot of celebrating later, Nellie thought — if the weather held, that is. The sky was darkening by the minute and the winds were growing stronger.

"Mr. Bromley has invited our whole team down to celebrate after they finish — so I guess I'll be going even though they didn't call me as a second," Jack said, looking sideways at his sister.

Nellie suspected he was trying to get a rise out of her. Maybe she'd been ribbing him a bit too much today. She did not reply but thought of Sarah again. Where had she and her mother gone? She hadn't seen them at the Methodist church. It was highly unlikely that they'd gone to the Presbyterian church during the break. And it was even less likely for them to have gone to the hotel.

"Miss Mooney!" Even before Nellie turned, she recognized Sarah's voice. And she knew by the high-pitched sound that something was wrong.

Sarah came up beside Nellie. "Ma can't . . . find . . . Pa," she blurted out breathlessly. "And our horses . . . are gone . . . from the hotel stable."

"Maybe your father's on his way down here to fetch you."

"No, he isn't."

Jack was looking at Sarah now. "You stay with Nellie and Barbara," he said, "while I go to help your mother." Then, turning to Nellie, he said, "This storm may break any minute, and the bonspiel will have to be rescheduled. If that happens, you and Barbara wait for me at the Methodist parsonage or the church. They'll have to keep it open. Some folks may not be able to make it home tonight if this storm is bad enough."

Then he turned to Barbara. "I'm sorry, Barbara. With the looks of this sky, I was just going to suggest I get you safely home. But I think I'd better go look for our neighbour. He may not be in any condition to cope with this weather."

"That's all right, Jack. I understand." She reached out for one of Jack's hands and squeezed it in both of hers. "Now, *you* take care of yourself, too."

Nellie knew that it took all one's wits to beat a bad Manitoba storm. And no person in his right mind would risk driving into one. So Mr. Sayers had to be found before the storm hit.

"Don't you worry, Sarah. I'll find your pa," Jack said. He turned and strode down the street to the shed where he had left his horses and sleigh.

****

"Won't you eat a bite, Mrs. Sayers?" Mrs. Ingram coaxed.

Jack had brought Mrs. Sayers back to the parsonage. The threatened storm had now broken fully, and he was out in the midst of it, hunting for her husband. Nellie felt hopeless. How could he succeed? The snow was flying so thickly it was impossible to see more than a short distance ahead.

For once, Mrs. Ingram was not saying much. But she did give Nellie a knowing stare and shook her head.

"No, not a bite," Mrs. Sayers said. "But Sarah here should eat."

"Then you'd better come on over here and set a good example," Mrs. Ingram urged. Mrs. Sayers stood up slowly and took her long-faced child over to the table with her.

It was six o'clock now. The games had been stopped just after Jack had left at two, and most people had rushed away, hoping to get home ahead of the storm.

The local people would be safe, but those from farther away would have had to find shelter. Nellie thought of her mother alone and was thankful that her brother Will and her brother-in-law, Tom, farmed so near. They'd promised to check on Mother and the cattle.

Nellie walked to the front hall of the parsonage

and looked out into the storm. It was easing up now, and as she stood there, she saw a flat sleigh coming up the street.

It was Jack. He drove right up to the church hitching post, tied his horses, and hurried over, red-faced from the cold and short of breath. Nellie grabbed her cloak and stepped outside.

"George Ingram and I have searched this town over. It's been slow going." Jack stopped to catch his breath. "We couldn't see at all for a time and had to stop for about an hour. That's when we checked out the hotel."

"I suppose he's been drinking."

"I'm afraid so. And he started right early this morning. He didn't watch the games at all. He was the only customer up at the bar then — according to John."

"But Mr. Bromley promised me he'd not sell him anything till noon!"

"I wasn't talking to him — just John. He'd sell liquor to his own grandmother. That fellow's got no scruples. It probably wasn't Bromley's fault."

"Well, he's responsible for his employees," Nellie shot back.

"Maybe Sayers has met with an accident. But I can't think he's in town, and it's strange that he'd head out home with the horses while his wife and Sarah were still here."

"When did John say he left the hotel?"

"He wasn't certain. Thinks it was about half an hour at least before the storm hit."

They both fell silent. "Barbara's waiting for you," Nellie said after a moment.

"There's no time to take her home now." Jack looked worried. "She can come with us. We'd better take Mrs. Sayers and Sarah home, and see if Sayers is there already. On the way, we can check in on Mother. Will plans to do our chores, and Mrs. Sayers may need help if her husband's in a state. Chances are he was too drunk to drive the horses, so they just took him home."

When Nellie called them, Barbara, Mrs. Sayers, and Sarah stepped out of the front hallway of the parsonage, where they'd been waiting.

"You go ahead, Jack," Barbara said. "The Moores said I could ride home with them. Mother will worry if I'm late. I hope you find Mr. Sayers soon."

Mrs. Sayers and Nellie crowded in beside Jack on the seat. Sarah sat at her mother's feet, her frightened eyes peeking over the edge of the buffalo robe.

It was slow going. The fresh snow was not packed yet, and Jack drove cautiously. He didn't want to get stuck. Intense cold was settling in all around.

About half an hour later, Nellie felt a lump rise in her throat as a light flickered in the distance. It was Mother's lamp, sitting in the kitchen window. She knew it would have blinked there through the whole afternoon, a beacon not only for them but for anyone caught in the storm.

A deep silence had fallen over all of them as the horses plodded through the snow. When they approached the farm lane, Jack broke out with, "Here, Nellie, hang onto the reins while I check on Mother. She'll know if Will's done the chores."

He jumped down and waded through the thick

snow towards the house. Nellie couldn't help thinking that if Will had been there, he would have taken time to shovel out the path. When the door closed behind Jack, Nellie turned to Sarah.

The young girl had thrown back the buffalo robe and was peering out from under it. "Are we home?" she asked.

"Almost," her mother said quietly. "We're at Nellie's." She spoke in a calm voice, but Nellie could see the fear in her eyes.

Sarah looked very close to tears. Nellie knew that if she did cry, the tears could freeze to her cheeks. So she turned to Mrs. Sayers. "We could leave Sarah with Mother for tonight."

"Are you certain your mother wouldn't mind?" Mrs. Sayers said with some relief.

"She'd be glad to have the company," Nellie said truthfully. She knew her mother would like nothing better than to feed the thin child.

"Sarah," Mrs. Sayers said, pulling back the buffalo robe, "would you like to stay with Mrs. Mooney tonight?"

"No!" Sarah was hysterical now. "I'm going home. I want to know if Pa's there." She disappeared under the robe again.

Mrs. Sayers' eyes came to life a little as she stared at the bump under the buffalo robe. "I think we'd better let her be," she said. "And she *is* company for me."

Nellie stared back at her in silence, trying not to think of what Sarah might see, now that she was going home. She was reminded that Mr. Sayers would be no company for anyone when they did find him. Nellie secretly hoped he'd be out cold, so he wouldn't try to beat up his wife. But this time, Jack would be there to protect them all.

Jack came out the back kitchen door and once again waded through the snow to the sleigh. "The chores are all done, but Will and Tom had to leave to get back to do their own chores before they got snowed in here. Tom brought Lizzie and little George to stay the night with Mother. Now, I've decided to change horses. This team's worn out. You can warm up a bit in the house or ride down to the barn with me."

"It'll be faster if we go with you," Mrs. Sayers said.

In less than ten minutes, they were on the road again, the two women and Sarah huddled under a pair of buffalo robes on the back of the sleigh. Pulled by a fresh team, they were travelling at a much faster speed. But the horses' harness bells, which Nellie generally loved to hear, seemed too loud.

When Nellie felt the sleigh turning, she threw back the robe. Mrs. Sayers was already sitting up straight and straining to see ahead, for they had turned into the Sayers' laneway.

"Jack! Are there any tracks ahead?" Nellie called out.

"No, but then they'd probably be covered up by the storm — I think I see something though," he said out of the side of his mouth as he strained to look ahead.

"What is it?"

"Movement . . . inside the shed." Jack drove them right up to the shed attached to the house.

The Sayers' team stood just inside, shaking with cold.

Mrs. Sayers jumped from the wagon and ran into the shed. Jack followed her and grabbed the reins of the cold horses, to quiet them down.

A scream pierced the air. "He's here!" Mrs. Sayers sobbed, bending over the front of the wagon.

Nellie looked down in horror. Mr. Sayers' face was a frozen mask. "Is he . . . is he? Oh, Jack!"

Jack was already lifting Mr. Sayers and pulling him towards the house. Mrs. Sayers and Nellie grabbed his feet while Sarah, whimpering, ran ahead and opened the door.

They laid Mr. Sayers on the red hooked mat by the kitchen stove. Jack felt for a pulse as he looked up at Mrs. Sayers' stone-white face. "I think there's a pulse," he said, "but it's very weak. You'd better bring blankets and stoke up that fire."

Mrs. Sayers flew to the bedroom for blankets, calling over her shoulder, "Get me some kindling, Sarah."

Sarah dug into the woodbox behind the stove for the small pieces. Tears were streaming down her face. "He'll be all right, won't he, Ma?" she asked.

Her mother took the kindling silently, placed it in the stove, lit it with a match, and opened the draft in the stovepipe. Then without looking at anyone else, she dropped down to the floor and knelt beside her husband.

"I'd best hurry for the doctor," Jack said. "But don't let him get warm too fast. I'm sure his feet and hands are frozen. Maybe his legs, too." Jack moved Mr. Sayers away from the stove a bit, keeping the red mat under him.

"I'll have to put the horses in the barn," he said. "If it gets any colder, they could freeze to death before I get back."

"You go for the doctor. I'll attend to the horses. I can't do much for Don," Mrs. Sayers said. She turned her desperate, pleading eyes on him. "Please hurry!" Then she rushed out.

Jack swallowed hard and bolted through the back door. In seconds, Nellie could hear the bells from the horses' harness as the sleigh pulled away on its smoothly worn runners.

Sarah crept over beside Nellie and together they looked at Sarah's father. His eyes, half-closed, stared up at them from a swollen white face, blotched with purple. Were his eyes not moving because they were frozen? Did he know or feel anything?

Sarah buried her face in her hands and started to sob loudly. Then she turned, walked to the foot of the ladder and climbed up to her bedroom in the loft. Nellie was alone with the frozen man. She shivered as she stared into his nearly unrecognizable face.

In a few minutes, Mrs. Sayers returned from the stable. She knelt down beside her husband and began to cry. Tears streamed down her face as she picked up Mr. Sayers' large left hand and started to rub it between her own two small ones.

"Oh, my dear, my dear," she cried. "You must come out of this, you must. How could I live without you?"

Nellie could watch no more. She went to the window and gazed outside. She was thankful to see that no more snow had fallen, but she knew that a deep cold had set in. She was glad that Lizzie had gone over to stay with her mother and watch the fire. This would be the worst night of the year to have stovepipes catch fire!

Nellie stopped herself. How could she be thinking of stovepipes when she was in a room with a man who was probably dead or dying? Sayers was as stiff as death, and his patchy coloured face was like nothing she had ever seen before.

Mrs. Sayers was shaking her husband's hands hysterically. "Look at me, my dear one, just once more," the woman was screaming at him. "You've been my whole life and a grand husband. I could never manage without you!"

Nellie thought of John, the assistant bartender, and all the grief he'd caused. And Mr. Bromley wasn't blameless either. She'd see that he paid — and all those other hotelkeepers, too. At the same time, she couldn't help being amazed at this woman's blind devotion to the man who had made her life miserable.

Nellie kept watching at the window for Jack. The wind was starting to lift and whirl the thick snow, creating white-outs in places.

She shivered and looked back at the forms on the floor, and then at the stove. The pipe was red-hot now. She hurried over to turn the damper and check the fire. They didn't need a stovepipe fire here, either.

Mrs. Sayers was still rocking back and forth on

her knees beside her husband and mumbling low, endearing terms. Nellie looked away from the pathetic sight, towards the ladder that led to the loft. She hadn't heard a sound from Sarah for some time now.

It was growing quite dark. The only light in the kitchen came from the hot stove lids. Nellie walked over to the foot of the ladder. "Sarah, will you please come down here and find a lamp for me to light?"

At first there was no sound, and Nellie thought the girl must have gone to sleep. So she turned back towards the kitchen cupboard. Just then, Sarah's feet and legs appeared at the top of the ladder.

Without speaking to Nellie, she came down and walked like a sleepwalker to the far side of the kitchen. She reached inside the cupboard and pulled out a lamp. She took off the glass shade, and lit a match. Then she put the flame to the wick and fit the glass shade back on. She turned the wick a bit lower, so the flame would not blacken the glass chimney, then handed the lamp to Nellie. A low, steady light flowed out as Nellie set it down on the table. Flickering shadows danced around the room.

"May I go now?" Sarah asked quietly.

"If you like," Nellie said. She knew that Sarah could not bear to look at her mother. The girl crawled back up the ladder again. This time, she closed the trap door.

Loud thumping steps were now coming towards the front of the house. Nellie hurried over and opened the door. Dr. Evans, the new young doctor from Wawanesa, pushed right into the room. He was tall like Wes, but with dark brown hair.

"Where's Jack?" Nellie asked.

"He's gone to get more men to help with the chores." The doctor handed his bag to Nellie and removed his raccoon coat. Throwing it over a chair, he said, "He's gone for a vet, too. Now, bring my bag along while I warm my hands. It's a cold night, and it's getting colder." He gave Nellie a bright smile and moved over to the stove.

The doctor held his hands over the stove for only a minute as he stared open-mouthed at the body on the floor and the hysterical woman. Mrs. Sayers had put her head on her husband's chest and was sobbing uncontrollably. Sayers' ghastly-coloured face lay uncovered, and the frozen eyes stared ahead.

"Mrs. Sayers," the doctor said quietly, leaning over, "I am Dr. Evans. I'm new in town. Dr. Small is delivering a baby tonight, so I came instead. It's terribly cold outside. Could you make me a warm cup of tea, please, while I examine your husband?"

Mrs. Sayers looked at him blankly. Nellie thought she was just going to stay there, but she suddenly jumped up and said, "Tea! Of course. I'll have it ready for you shortly."

Nellie knelt beside the doctor. He listened to the patient's heart for a long time. Then he shook his head and mumbled to Nellie, "He's been gone for some time now. Are you sure your brother found a heartbeat?"

"I thought he did," Nellie sighed. Maybe Jack

had just said that to break the news more easily. Nellie glanced across the room at Mrs. Sayers, who was cutting a fruit loaf. How were they going to tell her and Sarah?

The doctor stood up and waited until Mrs. Sayers brought the tea and cake to the table. When she saw them both looking at her, she knew.

With shaking hands, she set the tea on the table, rushed over, and dropped onto her knees beside her husband.

Dr. Evans squatted on the floor next to her and said, "He's gone now. It's doubtful that what Jack felt really was a pulse. And if your husband had managed to pull through, he would have been severely maimed. His limbs were frozen solid."

"Noooo!" she cried out as she grabbed her husband's frozen left hand in both of hers.

The sound of her mother's cry brought Sarah from the loft. She hurried down the ladder to kneel beside her father, wrapping her small arms around her mother's shoulders. Her thin frame shook with quiet, choking sobs.

14

"It's beautiful," Nellie said, staring at the photograph Sarah had just laid on her desk.

It was the last week of April. Nearly two months had passed since Sarah's father died. "I hope it will remind you of the happy times, Sarah, so you'll forget the sad ones."

Tears glistened in the girl's eyes as she said, "He was a kind father . . . when he wasn't drinking."

"Yes, I know." Nellie smiled gently.

"I've finished cleaning the boards, so I'd better hurry home, Miss Mooney," Sarah said, putting the photograph back in her satchel. "Ma needs me."

"Of course."

Nellie knew that Mrs. Brown had been helping Mrs. Sayers learn how to manage the farm. Jack and Will had found time to lend a hand, too, and were preparing her land for seeding. Of course, Mrs. Sayers would need to get a regular hired man before harvest time. But that wouldn't be difficult. And although her crop would not be as large as last year's, this year Mrs. Sayers would be able to keep all she earned. And Mr. Stead had cancelled the rent payment for at least twelve months.

"Grandpa liked the picture," Sarah said, "and Ma says we'll be visiting them for Christmas this year."

"How is your grandpa?"

"He's much better. Isn't it strange? We thought he was dying, and Pa died instead."

"Yes, it is strange." Nellie was thinking how unnecessary Mr. Sayers' death had been.

"Goodbye, Miss Mooney," Sarah said. Her bag packed, she hurried out of the school.

After a few moments, Nellie took out her latest letter from Wes. She flipped over the pages to its final words.

I'm coming home right after the exams. It's been so long, and I need to see you, Nellie. It's been too long since we've seen each other. I need to be with you again to make sure that you are real. I look at your picture every day but that's not good enough!

I think I'm in love with you, Nellie, but then am I really? Or am I in love with your picture and your letters? I need to see you Nellie and soon — before you fade away from me. I need to feel that great sense of well-being that I have when I am with you. With your enthusiasm and your love of life, you light all the candles of my mind. I long to be with you again, to see if the old

*spark is still there between us, as it has always been. I'll
be coming to see you as soon as I can.*

Till then, please wait for me.
As ever,

> *Lovingly,*
> *Wes.*

Nellie folded the letter and put it back in her
purse. Wes had written it three weeks before, and
she knew that his examinations were over now.
Would he wait there for his results or catch a train
right home? She couldn't guess.

But she did know he was coming — and to her
home, for the first time, really. Though Wes and
his sister had stopped by the summer before to
take Nellie back to Manitou with them, Wes
hadn't even come into the house. Mother wasn't
even aware how close the two of them were.

So Wes was finally going to pay his first real visit
to the farm. What would he think of her folks?
Would he look down on them because they ate in
the kitchen and in their shirt-sleeves? Or would he
see them as she did — clear thinking, independent people, more ready to give a favour than ask
for one?

And what about Mother? Nellie wondered.
Would he see what a good woman she was? For all
her bluntness, she had a gracious spirit, and knew
the healing word for souls in distress. She scorned
pretence and affectation, and loved the sweet and
simple virtues. No night was too dark or cold, no
road too dangerous for her to go out and help a
neighbour in need.

Would Wes see all this? Or would there be a trace of condescension in his manner, that even he might be unaware of?

With a sigh, Nellie packed up her books. It was Friday again, but she would put the lessons on the board on Monday morning.

She stroked Bess gently before she lifted the sidesaddle onto her back. Already the field around the schoolyard was a pattern of open furrows of rich dark soil, ready for seeding.

Along the road home, Nellie felt the pulsing of new life that comes in the spring of the year. Pussy willows were standing tall in a stream by the roadside, and warm breezes ruffled the bushes. The air had a freshness that was invigorating.

In the distance, she heard a train whistle. Looking back over her shoulder to the east, she thought she saw smoke billowing in the distance. She had always loved trains — the way they pounded the rails, screaming out signals and ringing their bells. They were something like the spring, for both brought her energy and filled her with the joy of living.

At the foot of the lane to the Mooney farm, Nellie drew off the saddle and gave Bess a pat on the rump to send her running to the pasture. Then she set the saddle and her school bag beside the fence and ran downhill to the creek below the house.

She leaned over and picked a large bouquet of pussy willows. Then, dropping them on the damp ground beside her, she sat on a small stone and gazed out across the creek at the land she loved.

She would be leaving it this fall, for she had applied for a school in Winnipeg. But it would always be her homeland.

She was free to leave, at last. Lizzie had asked Mother to move in with her and Tom, now that Jack was planning to be married in the fall.

In Winnipeg, Nellie would start writing her novel. This year, there had hardly been time for *reading* novels, let alone writing them. As Father had always said, Mother could keep forty people busy. There was never an end to the work around the house.

Nellie couldn't wait to tell Wes her plans. "Next September, I'll move to Winnipeg to teach," she would say, "and I'll join the WCTU there. I'll learn from these women and become more active. And Wes, I'll write a novel. I *know* I can write. There are so many people I want to put in my stories — the real people who do the work of the world. And, Wes, I'll write it from their side of the fence. I'll show the world how hard their lives are and how brave they are, too."

Nellie sighed as she looked towards the vacant spot beside her on the knoll, where she'd imagined Wes was sitting.

Mother would be expecting her to be in the house about now, getting ready to prepare supper. So Nellie stood up and ran up the knoll to the house. When I'm working in Winnipeg, she thought, I'll find a boarding house with all meals provided.

"I'm home," Nellie called out as she walked in and threw her bag down on the chair under the coat-pegs. There was no response. Mother was nowhere to be seen. There was no roaring fire or steaming kettle. The table hadn't even been set!

Nellie couldn't imagine why her mother would be away from the kitchen at this hour. The clock showed a quarter after five — past time to start preparing the evening meal. Had something happened to Mother?

Just then Nellie heard voices coming from the other room. Mother and . . . Her heart thumped. It was Wes!

Nellie stepped into the front room. Wes was sitting by the window, the afternoon sun shining across his auburn hair and lighting up his strong features. He stood when he saw her, tall and straight as ever, but a little thin and pale in his rough tweed suit.

"Well, young lady, I hear you've been corresponding with this young man for some time," Mrs. Mooney said. "We've been having a grand chat. I didn't know you'd have such good sense in picking a young man."

"Mother, I . . ." Nellie was embarrassed by her mother's comments. What would Wes think? That she'd said he'd proposed? Or that she didn't care enough about him to tell her mother about their letters? Then again, he couldn't think both. Nellie was so confused. But, oh, how good it was to see Wes. She knew now how much she'd missed him.

"Well, why don't you two have a walk while I prepare supper? I'm sure you have a lot to discuss." Mrs. Mooney hurried out to the kitchen.

"I'd like that," Wes said, smiling at Nellie, whose

cheeks were turning crimson.

The whole countryside seemed alive with sound as Nellie and Wes walked down the knoll through the blue anemones that carpeted the countryside. A meadowlark broke into a sweet song and the creek gurgled at their feet.

They sat down together on a large dry stone, the silence hanging heavy between them. Nellie looked up at Wes beside her. He was gazing across the creek to a distant place. Was he thinking of those other women, or even one woman, he'd met in Toronto? Was he trying to think how he would tell her?

"Wes?" she blurted out and then fell silent. For once, she must not speak. She would accept whatever he had to say and make the best of it. She knew now that she loved this tall, silent man who sat beside her, but she knew, too, that she would take it bravely on the chin if he had found someone else.

"I can't tell you how glad I am to be back home with the people I love, Nellie," Wes began.

He had used the word "love." Did he mean her? Or his family? "I've missed you, too, Wes," she said, irritating herself with her own calm voice. She sounded as if her feelings for him were routine, when actually she longed for this strong, quiet man to reach out for her. If he did, she knew she would fold her arms around him in a way that would leave no doubt about her feelings.

But he had to make the first move. She would not be able to stand the rejection, the surprise and hurt in those clear blue eyes if he knew her feelings and was unable to return them.

"It's all becoming real, again, Nellie," he said. "It never was unreal. I just was away so long. But nothing has changed. And most of all, you're the same wonderful person. In fact, I think we know each other better now because of our letters. Sometimes, we hesitate to put into spoken words what we will write in letters."

Wes got up and came around and squatted in front of Nellie. He took Nellie's hand. She smiled down at him, but her heart was beating rapidly while she was thinking — his letters! Did his letters contain his deepest thoughts? He didn't propose marriage in his letters!

But before she could despair, she gazed into Wes's serious eyes and saw an expression that she had never seen there before. She gave a short little gasp and waited.

"But there are some things that one can't write about . . . that one needs to do in person. I hope I'm saying this right, Nellie. What I'm trying to say is that . . . I know now. I'm certain I love you and only *you*. Nellie, if only you would feel the same way. I shouldn't have waited so long to tell you, but I just couldn't do it when I was so many miles away."

"Oh, Wes," Nellie almost shouted with glee as she gazed lovingly down into the depths of his steady eyes and reached out towards him.

Wes took both of her small hands in his big ones and looked up at her humbly. "I want to marry you and spend my life with you," he said. "And, Nellie," he went on, "if only you'll have me, I promise I'll never interfere with your work . . ." He stopped, almost breathless. His clear blue eyes looked straight into her bright brown ones.

"Yes, Wes, I'll marry you," Nellie said as she slid off the rock and wrapped her arms around him. She lifted her face to his and their lips met.

A few minutes later, hand in hand, they walked slowly back up the hill to the kitchen door, where Jack stood watching them. "I knew there was a reason you were so obliging about getting our mail all the time!" he said.

Wes gave a hearty laugh, and reached out his hand to Jack. "It's nice to see you again, Jack." He smiled at Mother. "You weren't even expecting a visitor and you've put on such a marvellous meal!" He was gazing at the kitchen table, as though it were a banquet.

He was fitting right in, Nellie decided, like the last piece of a puzzle.

After the meal, they talked in the front room for a while, then Jack finally remembered he had chores to do. After he had left for the barn, he opened the door and called back inside, "It's a beautiful night." There was a twinkle in his eye.

"I haven't been home yet," Wes said to Mother and Nellie. "I rented a horse and buggy from the livery stable to come here, but Father is meeting me tonight at Wawanesa. I hate to leave now, but I must, or he'll think I missed the train."

Nellie smiled and nodded.

"Thank you for the wonderful supper, Mrs. Mooney."

"You're more than welcome, young man. I'm expecting you'll be back soon. I love to cook for a man with a good appetite."

As they stepped out into the night, Wes reached over and took Nellie's hand in his. The moon shone across the pathway as they walked down to the horse and buggy tied at the end of the lane by the road.

"Nellie?"

"Yes, Wes."

"If you're free on Saturday, I'd like to come back in the morning, to take you to Winnipeg to pick out a ring."

"Oh, Wes, I'd love that."

"And I'm going to buy the little drugstore in Manitou. I don't have any money, but it's all to be arranged through the bank. So I'd like to marry you this summer. I'll have enough to support us."

They both knew that Nellie would have to give up teaching, for she would not be hired by any school board while she had a husband to support her.

"August would be a lovely time to be married," Nellie said. "That'll give me July to prepare to set up housekeeping." She hadn't even thought about a hope chest, as most other girls had, but then what did that matter?

Hesitating at the buggy, Wes bent down a bit and wrapped his arms around her. Impulsively, she threw both of her arms around his neck and kissed him on the lips. Then, finally, Wes turned and stepped up into the buggy.

Nellie stood there and waved until Wes was out of sight down the road. Then she walked slowly back up to the house with the moonlight streaming across her pathway.

As Nellie was getting ready for bed, Mother came into her room. "Nellie," she said, "you have more sense than I've given you credit for — and you certainly are getting something to look at, as you always said you would. I like your young man — I couldn't have picked a finer one, myself. Now, if you cannot get on, I'll be inclined to think it will be your fault."

Nellie chuckled after Mother left the room. As ever, she gave the men she liked all the credit. Then to herself, Nellie mumbled, "I'm glad you like Wes, Mother, but someday, I'll make my own mark. And I'm glad *Wes* doesn't think of me as a looking glass."

Notes

Most of the incidents in *Nellie's Quest* are true, but dramatized and enhanced with fictional detail to bring them to life. This novel is based on Nellie L. McClung's autobiographies, *Clearing in the West* and *The Stream Runs Fast*, and follows these volumes very closely.

Nellie's work in the Women's Christian Temperance Union led her to the Political Equality League, which sought the vote for women in Manitoba. She reasoned that when women received the vote, prohibition would follow. She soon realized, however, that women in Canada and elsewhere suffered from many other forms of inhumanity. This only served to reinforce her fervour in fighting for women's votes.

In her autobiographies and in her fictional

writing there are several incidents describing drunken men who brought hardship and often disaster upon the women in their lives. I have chosen two of these for this novel — one who reformed and one who did not. In *The Stream Runs Fast* (p.62), Nellie says that "elsewhere I have written the story of the woman and her little girl who were disappointed in their trip to Ontario." "Elsewhere" is Nellie L. McClung's second novel, *The Second Chance*, where the drunken Bill Cavers spends on alcohol the money he had promised to his wife and child for a visit to her home in Ontario. Then the following summer, in a drunken state at a picnic, he died of sun exposure before their family picture was taken. You will recognize similarities to my story about the Sayers family.

Nellie describes the conversion of Silas Brand (the source for the Mr. Wheeler character), who truly was converted at the Judd sisters' meetings, in *Clearing in the West* (pgs. 298-99). The description in *Clearing* is inspired by Nellie's receiving Silas's obituary notice from one of his sons about forty years after the conversion. This obituary, written by the United Church minister in Wawanesa, said, "He was soundly converted many years ago, in revival meetings conducted by the Misses Judd, in Manitou, and his zeal for the work of God knew no languor. His memory in this neighbourhood will ever be a happy one."

The following quotes (which have been included in *Nellie's Quest*) were taken from *Clearing in the West*, unless otherwise noted. Occasionally, I have changed a quote slightly to make it more readable

for today's students. In some cases, I have made
more significant changes in Nellie's language.
These also are indicated below. The numbers in
the left column refer to the pages in *Nellie's Quest*.

16   The lives of these country people . . . excitement
       and change. (paraphrase): Nellie L. McClung in
       The Stream Runs Fast 59.

28   "The Irish people . . . to keep their hearts from
       breaking.": Mr. Mooney 36.

28   "I'm glad you are Irish.": Nellie 36.

29   "Shule, shule . . . me bread.": Mr. Mooney 37.

31   "black goatskin shoes . . . peeled . . . gaping a bit
       at the top.": Nellie 303.

46   "Mother had . . . Old World reverence for men.":
       Nellie 257.

60   It was a hammock . . . till next spring, Nellie
       thought. (paraphrase): Nellie 351.

62   He has denounced governments . . . the traffic in
       liquor. (paraphrase): Nellie 344.

62   made only to . . . inspire men: Ruskin, in *Sesame
       and Lilies*, qtd. in *Clearing in the West* 283.

63   "men like quiet women" Nellie 283.

64   "There are too many of us . . . it makes her
       mad.": Evadell [Jane] 355.

64-65 "She . . . see[s] you here . . . if you knew.":
       Evadell [Jane] 355.

67   "Of course, I know . . . you'll be some day.":
       Evadell's [Jane's] mother 356.

78   "I didn't think . . . stronger mind than yours":
       Nell 349.

83   "She of the . . ." construction used by Nellie
       McClung in *The Stream Runs Fast* 96.

83-84 "The church does . . . appeals to the best in
       human nature.": Nellie in *The Stream Runs Fast* 71.

84   "helping to shape society to change lives for the better.": Nellie in *The Stream Runs Fast* 72.

84   "God was good at forgetting." Mr. Mooney 67.

84   Ruskin's *Sesame and Lilies* . . . well-folded table-cloths. (paraphrase): Nellie 283.

86   "sweet, placid, serene . . . above earth's lamentation": Nellie 353.

104   "Softly and . . . for me.": hymn at Judd sisters' meeting 295.

105   "had a face . . . blue flame.": Nellie 294.

105   "Maude . . . of this earth.": Nellie 294.

105   "Her eyes . . . dark lilacs [pansy].": Nellie 294.

105   "reddish brown rough tweed . . . and sleeves.": Nellie 295.

105   "Nettie's soprano voice . . . like [a cello] an organ.": Nellie 294-95.

105   "Come home . . . come home.": hymn at the Judd sisters' meeting 295.

105-06 "We do well to be excited over the greatest thing in life. Religion is greater . . . amongst you?": Hettie Judd 297.

107   "such a tall, pale husk of a woman . . . a [scarecrow] clothes horse.": Nellie 298.

108   "a lazy [good-for-nothing] letting my wife support [me] . . . a long suffering angel.": Silas Brand (Wheeler) 298.

108   "so help me God.": Brand (Wheeler) 298.

117   "I knew nothing of business until my husband died.": Mrs. Brown 305.

117   "had to do a man's work . . . and in doing that": Mrs. Brown 305.

117   "Men are afraid of women, jealous of them, and unfair to them. They want women to be looking-glasses for them [though] false ones [to] make them look bigger than they are.": Nellie L. McClung through Mrs. Brown 305.

quote): Nellie 356.

167   "[Wes] was a fair fighter . . . than agree with any-
       one else.": Nellie 375.

184   "light all the candles of my mind.": Nellie 354.

185   "Would he look down on . . . shirt sleeves?":
       Nellie 375.

185   "Or would he see them as [she] did . . . than ask
       for one.": Nellie 375.

185   And what about Mother? . . . a neighbour in dis-
       tress. (paraphrase): Nellie 375.

186   "see all this . . . be unaware": Nellie 375.

186   "trains . . . pounded the rails . . screaming out
       their signals and ringing their bells.": Nellie 321.

186   "fill[ed her] with joy of living": Nellie McClung
       321.

187   The real people who do the work . . . really are
       too. (paraphrase): Nellie 226.

191   "like the last piece of a . . . puzzle.": Nellie
       McClung 375.

193   "Nellie, you have more sense . . . it will be your
       fault.": Mrs. Mooney 375, 376.

CONNIE BRUMMEL CROOK

Connie B. Crook was born near Belleville, Ontario, during the Depression. As a child she had to walk more than a mile no matter the weather to her one-room primary school, and later three miles to her high school. When she grew up she taught English in several secondary schools across the province.

Although Ms. Crook has always loved writing, she didn't' get a chance to pursue it until her recent retirement. Now living in Peterborough, Ontario, she spends her time writing, visiting schools, walking, swimming, reading, and babysitting her five grandchildren, including her twin grandsons, who used to play the part of Daniel King in the popular television series *Road to Avonlea*.